Mission Statement

Created more than twenty years ago
by James Colby, the Colby Agency is now
owned and operated by his wife, Victoria.
Though relatively small, the agency has garnered
a reputation second to none in the business of
private investigations and personal security.
Victoria Colby is highly respected by law
enforcement and is well connected in government
agencies where *discretion* is the operative word.

The Colby Agency employs the very finest in all
aspects of investigation and protection. Each of
the men and women who represents the agency
must possess the qualities that James Colby
himself personified: honor, loyalty and courage.

The Colby Agency is the place where clients go
when only the absolute best will do.

Dear Harlequin Intrigue Reader,

We've got another month of sinister summer sizzlers lined up for you starting with the one and only Familiar—your favorite crime-solving black cat! Travel with the feisty feline on a magic carpet to the enchanting land of sheiks in Caroline Burnes's *Familiar Mirage*, the first part of FEAR FAMILIAR: DESERT MYSTERIES. You can look for the companion book, *Familiar Oasis*, next month.

Then it's back to the heart of the U.S.A. for another outstanding CONFIDENTIAL installment. This time, the sexiest undercover operatives around take on Chicago in this bestselling continuity series. Cassie Miles launches the whole shebang with *Not on His Watch*.

Debra Webb continues her COLBY AGENCY series with one more high-action, heart-pounding romantic suspense story in *Physical Evidence*. What these Colby agents won't do to solve a case—they'll even become prime suspects to take care of business...and fall in love.

Finally, esteemed Harlequin Intrigue author Leona Karr brings you a classic mystery about a woman who washes up on the shore sans memory. Good thing she's saved by a man determined to find her *Lost Identity*.

A great lineup to be sure. So make sure you pick up all four titles for the full Harlequin Intrigue reading experience.

Sincerely,

Denise O'Sullivan
Associate Senior Editor
Harlequin Intrigue

PHYSICAL EVIDENCE
DEBRA WEBB

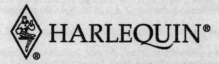

TORONTO • NEW YORK • LONDON
AMSTERDAM • PARIS • SYDNEY • HAMBURG
STOCKHOLM • ATHENS • TOKYO • MILAN • MADRID
PRAGUE • WARSAW • BUDAPEST • AUCKLAND

ISBN 0-373-22671-3

PHYSICAL EVIDENCE

Copyright © 2002 by Debra Webb

This edition published by arrangement with Harlequin Books S.A.

® and TM are trademarks of the publisher. Trademarks indicated with ® are registered in the United States Patent and Trademark Office, the Canadian Trade Marks Office and in other countries.

Visit us at www.eHarlequin.com

Printed in U.S.A.

ABOUT THE AUTHOR

Debra Webb was born in Scottsboro, Alabama, to parents who taught her that anything is possible if you want it bad enough. She began writing at age nine. Eventually she met and married the man of her dreams and tried some other occupations, including selling vacuum cleaners, working in a factory, a day care center, a hospital and a department store. When her husband joined the military, they moved to Berlin, Germany, and Debra became a secretary in the commanding general's office. By 1985 they were back in the States, and they finally moved to Tennessee, to a small town where everyone knows everyone else. With the support of her husband and two beautiful daughters, Debra took up writing again, looking to mystery and movies for inspiration. In 1998 her dream of writing for Harlequin came true. You can write to Debra with your comments at P.O. Box 64, Huntland, Tennessee 37345.

Books by Debra Webb

HARLEQUIN INTRIGUE
583—SAFE BY HIS SIDE*
597—THE BODYGUARD'S BABY*
610—PROTECTIVE CUSTODY*
634—SPECIAL ASSIGNMENT: BABY
646—SOLITARY SOLDIER*
659—PERSONAL PROTECTOR*
671—PHYSICAL EVIDENCE*

*Colby Agency

HARLEQUIN AMERICAN ROMANCE
864—LONGWALKER'S CHILD

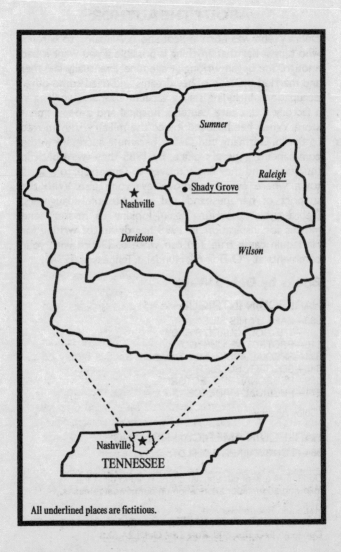

Sumner

Raleigh

Nashville ★

● Shady Grove

Davidson

Wilson

Nashville ★

TENNESSEE

All underlined places are fictitious.

CAST OF CHARACTERS

Alexandra Preston—Trained at Quantico, Alex is one of Victoria Colby's top investigators. Someone wants her dead, but she can't remember who or why.

Mitch Hayden—Sheriff of Raleigh County, Tennessee. His attraction to Alex Preston makes him question his deepest loyalty of all—family ties.

Victoria Colby—The head of the Colby Agency.

Zach Ashton—Victoria Colby's top legal eagle.

Deputy Miller—He was found dead in the car with Alex, who can't remember what happened. Was Miller trying to give her information or was he trying to shut her up before things went awry?

Phillip Malloy—He has a dirty little secret. Just how far will he go to protect it?

Nadine Malloy—Phillip's faithful wife. She doesn't need this case rocking her already-shaky emotional state. She will do whatever it takes to protect her family.

Roy Becker—A deputy who is also Mitch's cousin. As Phillip's stepson, Roy doesn't want his family hurt. But does he know something he's not telling?

Marija and Jasna Bukovak—Foreign exchange students from Croatia. Jasna has been attending the university in Chicago. As a high school senior, Marija has lived with the Malloys for the past school year. Shortly after graduation she disappeared.

Agent Talkington—The Tennessee Bureau of Investigation agent assigned to investigate a series of murders.

Waylon Gill—A serial killer thought to be responsible for the disappearance of Marija Bukovak.

This book is dedicated to a very special lady
who has had a tremendous influence on my writing
career. She recognized a diamond in the rough and
set to the task of cutting and polishing. It took hard
work and perseverance, but she never once gave up.
Since we met in 1996, she has made me laugh at myself,
cry because I was certain I could never do this writing
thing and swell with pride when I knew the work was
indeed good. This one is for you, Dianne Hamilton.
For all your selfless giving, for your every word
of encouragement and simply for being you.

Prologue

Victoria Colby watched the early morning commuters on the busy street beyond the parking lot four stories below. Deep inside, where she harbored her most secret thoughts and feelings, she knew something was very wrong. This September morning would bring bad news. She could feel it in her bones.

Drawing in a deep breath, she considered that she had worked hard since her husband's death to make the Colby Agency the best in the business. She employed only the very finest in the fields of research and investigation. She knew better than most that no amount of planning or strategy could ward off the unexpected twists and turns life took.

A soft knock on her office door pulled Victoria's attention back to the present. She stiffened her spine and turned to greet the attorney she had summoned so early this morning.

Zach Ashton entered the office, his expression nothing short of grim. "Is Hayden here yet?"

"Not yet." Victoria gestured to one of the wing back chairs flanking her desk as she settled into her own. She braced herself for Zach's report. "Have you been able to reach Alex?"

He shook his head slowly from side to side. "I've called at least a dozen times in the past two hours with no luck." He looked away briefly, and Victoria knew that he was having difficulty considering the possibilities of why Alex had not called in. "I couldn't reach the Bukovak girl either."

An uncharacteristic feeling of helplessness welled in Victoria's chest. The sensation was not completely foreign to her; she had known it well during the long months immediately following her husband's death. And she'd known it another time that she refused to consider even after all these years. Doggedly pushing it aside, she leveled a determined gaze on her trusted attorney. "We'll have some answers when Sheriff Hayden arrives."

Zach stared at the floor for a long moment. Victoria knew that he was assessing the situation and reaching the same conclusions she had. And the bottom line was not good, but neither of them was willing to admit that fact just yet.

Alexandra Preston had worked at the Colby Agency almost as long as Zach. She was very good at her job. Trained at Quantico as a special agent for the FBI, Alex was nobody's fool. She was attractive, smart and tough. But now she was missing in action. They'd had no contact with her in forty-eight hours. No one stayed out of touch that long unless they were stranded without communications, severely injured…or worse.

Victoria wished she could have saved Zach from this gut-wrenching wait, but he knew Alex better than anyone else in the agency. Victoria needed his input. Usually she avoided teaming two people who had been involved on a personal level, but whatever had been between Zach and Alex was over long ago. Both appeared to have moved on, but they remained close friends. And right now Alex needed Zach on her team, just as Victoria needed his expertise in the upcoming meeting.

Zach lifted a worried gaze to meet Victoria's. "We could be looking at a very bad situation here. Maybe there's someone else you'd rather have making assessments. I'm not sure I can be objective. If this is bad news…" His words drifted off to be replaced by a too-solemn silence.

Victoria considered her own words for a long moment before she spoke. "We can only hope for the best, but I doubt that the sheriff from Raleigh County, Tennessee, would drop everything and fly up without strong motivation. As to your involvement, I believe you're the best man for the job."

The intercom interrupted whatever Zach intended to say next. "Sheriff Hayden is here," Mildred announced.

"Show him in, please." Victoria stood, as did Zach, to welcome the man who had gotten her up at the crack of dawn to demand a meeting.

Sheriff Mitchell Hayden strode across Victoria's office without hesitating until he stood directly in front of her desk. The first thing that garnered her attention was his too-long hair, which was secured at the back of his neck. The next thing she noted was intense, cool blue eyes.

He extended his hand. "I'm Mitch Hayden, Mrs. Colby. Thank you for seeing me."

His deep, whiskey-smooth voice carried a hint of an unmistakable southern drawl. He was tall, six-one or two, she surmised. And solidly built. Victoria resisted the urge to frown when she considered his faded jeans and khaki shirt. The work boots didn't quite fit the bill either. She couldn't recall meeting a lawman who looked quite like this one.

"Sheriff Hayden," Victoria acknowledged as she gave his hand a brisk shake. "This is Zach Ashton, the agency's attorney."

Already standing, Zach clasped their visitor's hand next. "I hope your flight was pleasant, Sheriff."

"It was fine," he said curtly, then turned his attention back to Victoria. "I have several questions that need answers."

"Make yourself comfortable, Sheriff." She indicated the chair adjacent to Zach's as she resumed her own. "Why don't you tell me what brings you to Chicago this morning."

The sheriff's posture didn't relax as he sank into the seat she'd offered. He was intent, poised for whatever came his way. "Why does your agency have an investigator nosing around in my county?" he asked bluntly.

"If you mean Alex Preston, you're right, she is one of my investigators," Victoria acknowledged. "However, you must be aware that the information regarding the case she is working is private, Sheriff. Was there anything else you wanted to know?"

Only the slightest tightening of his jaw gave away Mitch Hayden's irritation. Victoria was impressed. The man had traveled a considerable distance to get stonewalled in the first two minutes.

"Don't jerk me around, Mrs. Colby," he warned. "I've been up all night and I've come a long way. I need some answers."

"Are you here because Alex is in some sort of trouble?" Zach asked pointedly, his courtroom demeanor going a long way to hide his anxiety.

An unbearable silence hung for two long beats.

"I think you already know the answer to that question," the sheriff replied quietly. Too quietly.

"If something has happened to Alex," Victoria countered firmly, "I demand that you tell us now."

He leveled an unreadable gaze fully onto Victoria's. "One of my deputies is dead, and Alex Preston is in the hospital under protective custody. She's also my prime suspect."

Mitch knew he'd gotten their full attention with that announcement. The attorney looked downright sick to his stomach, but the woman, Victoria Colby, seemed almost relieved, as if she'd feared worse. Maybe now Mitch would get some straight answers.

"What happened?" the attorney, Ashton, wanted to know.

"Is Alex all right?" Mrs. Colby demanded.

"She's fine other than having trouble remembering what happened," Mitch explained with as little detail as possible. "The two were found in Deputy Miller's car early yesterday morning by a group of kids who'd camped nearby. Miller was dead. It looks as if they shot each other. There was cocaine in the vehicle." Mitch paused, allowing them to absorb the ramifications of his words. "If you want to help clear her of a murder charge, I'd suggest that you start talking."

"I can assure you, Sheriff Hayden," Mrs. Colby said, more calmly than he would have expected, "that our investigation has nothing to do with drugs, nor is Alex a drug user."

"You're skirting the issue," Mitch snapped. His impatience was showing he knew, but at this point he didn't really give a damn.

"And you aren't?" she returned.

This was pointless. "I can get a warrant."

Mrs. Colby smiled. "Just so you know, Zach is one of the finest attorneys in the country. You may be in for a long wait."

"Is that a threat?"

"Absolutely not," Zach said emphatically, offering the sheriff his best, practiced smile. "Just fair warning."

Mitch suppressed the curse that raced to the tip of his tongue. "Look, I want to get to the bottom of this just as much as you do. And, like you, I know my men. Deputy Miller would never have shot anyone unless it was in self-defense and *he* sure as hell wasn't involved in drugs."

"Sheriff Hayden, I can assure you that we will do whatever it takes to help you determine what happened," Mrs. Colby offered.

Mitch knew she meant it. He had the distinct impression that Victoria Colby was a woman of her word. But the last thing he needed was further involvement from a civilian agency. All he wanted at the moment was answers.

"So." Mitch relaxed for the first time in more than twenty-four hours. "Does that mean you're ready to cooperate?"

"Only if you're ready to cooperate with us," she offered frankly.

Mitch inclined his head and considered the no-nonsense lady seated behind the big oak desk. "What will it take to get the information I need now? *Today.*"

"If your office cooperates completely with mine, then I'll return the favor," she explained. "Considering the geography, I would request that one of my people accompany you back to Tennessee. I want a full report on Alex's well-being. I would also require that my representative be allowed to participate in every aspect of the investigation to clear her name.''

"Is that all?'' Mitch asked sarcastically.

She dipped her head in a gesture of acknowledgment. "I believe that will be sufficient.''

Mitch let go a heavy breath. It crossed his mind to simply say no, but he had the feeling that Victoria Colby would not give in quite so easily. She would hold back the information he desperately needed until some judge made her give it up. He didn't want to waste time. Miller was dead. He'd been a friend as well as one of Mitch's best deputies. Mitch had every intention of solving this case as quickly as possible. Nothing, not Victoria Colby or her fancy agency, was going to stop him.

"All right, Mrs. Colby. Tell your man to be ready in three hours. That's when my flight leaves. Now—'' Mitch leaned forward in anticipation ''—will you give me the details regarding Alex Preston's case?''

"Certainly,'' Mrs. Colby said in an accommodating tone. "Zach will fill you in on the way. There's no need for you to wait three hours. I'll have my pilot take the two of you back to Nashville in the agency jet.''

Agency jet? Mitch tamped down his surprise, but couldn't suppress his renewed irritation. She was hedging again. "The case, Mrs. Colby,'' he insisted. "Tell me about the case.''

She stood, effectively dismissing him. "Zach will answer your questions en route. I want him with Alex ASAP. She's entitled to legal representation.''

Frowning, Mitch pushed hesitantly to his feet. Just what he needed, some hotshot, smart-mouth attorney dogging his every step. Especially one who looked ready to rip off Mitch's head and spit down his throat. "I'm not sure—"

"I'm sorry to interrupt," the secretary announced from the door. "But there's an urgent call for Sheriff Hayden."

Mrs. Colby pushed the telephone on her desk in his direction. "You can take it here, Sheriff."

Tired and annoyed, and definitely not up for any more problems, Mitch snatched up the receiver and depressed the blinking button. "Hayden." It was Russ Dixon, one of his deputies. "Slow down, Dixon, and tell me what the problem is." The deputy's next words stunned Mitch. A mixture of fury and anxiety clenched his gut. "I'm on my way," he said tightly and hung up.

"Is there a problem, Sheriff?" Mrs. Colby studied him closely, as if reading the new worry even before he spoke.

"That was one of my men," Mitch said, his voice oddly devoid of inflection. "Alex Preston is missing, and the deputy who was watching her is dead."

Chapter One

"The first shot entered here." Deputy Dixon pointed to one of the bullet holes in the hospital window.

Mitch Hayden stared at the entry hole and the spiderweb of cracked glass around it. "It must have come from the hotel across the street," he suggested, thinking out loud. The rooms in the four-story hotel had balconies with glass slider doors. Heavy curtains draped each set of sliders, offering excellent cover and the perfect angle for a shooter.

"That's what I figured," Dixon agreed. "The first round is the one that most likely hit the pillow right where Miss Preston would have laid her head. She apparently scrambled for cover, knocking over the telephone."

A muttered curse from near the bed dragged Mitch's attention in that direction. Zach Ashton, the Colby Agency's hotshot attorney, stood, staring down at the thin, disposable pillow that sported the nice round bullet hole.

Ashton lifted his gaze, meeting Mitch's. "She must have rolled over or gotten up at just the right moment," he surmised grimly, an underlying emotion in his tone that went beyond that of mere professional concern for a co-worker.

Without comment, Mitch turned back to Dixon so that he could continue with his scenario.

"The sound most likely alerted Saylor and he rushed into the room. Or maybe she screamed." Dixon indicated the second hole in the glass. "This round hit him dead center of his chest."

Dead being the operative word. Clenching his jaw to stave off the emotions tugging at him, Mitch glanced to the place where his deputy had fallen. Midway between the door and the bed, Saylor had lost his life.

Apparently thinking along the same vein, Ashton studied the handprint of dried blood on the floor next to where Saylor had been found.

"We figure Ms. Preston rolled off the bed on that side." Dixon gestured to the far side where Ashton stood. "Maybe to take cover or maybe to help Saylor. The bloody hand print on the floor isn't Saylor's or any of the hospital staff's. We think maybe she tried to stop the bleeding or give him CPR or something."

The deputy's words evolved into a fully formed scene in Mitch's head. The image of Alex Preston kneeling over Saylor attempting to stop the heavy flow of blood from his chest twisted the knot in Mitch's gut a few more turns.

"Good work, Dixon." Mitch started to turn away from the window, but hesitated. "Did you have a look over in the hotel already?"

"Sure did." Dixon pulled a small notepad from his shirt pocket. "Roy and Willis combed the entire building and even the trees accessible on this side of the hospital." Dixon shook his head. "They didn't find anything. We've interviewed dozens of people and no

one seems to have seen or heard anything suspicious."
He sighed. "It's like our shooter just plain vanished
into thin air."

Mitch scrubbed a hand over his face and tried to stay
fixed on the conversation when his mind wanted to
focus on the search for Alex, but he had to take care
of this first. "Well, we know he didn't just disappear.
We'll have to look harder that's all. Somebody had to
have seen or heard something." He glanced at his
watch. The shooting had taken place approximately
four hours ago. "I want every volunteer we can get out
there beating the bushes. I want her found before
dark."

"We've got most of our men, a big hunk of the
city's force, and a dozen or so volunteers out searching
already," Dixon assured him. "If she's still here, we'll
find her."

"That's what I want to hear." Mitch made a quick
mental checklist of all he had to do. "Ashton and I'll
join the search after I stop at the office. You make sure
this crime scene stays clean. TBI's techs may need to
go over the place again." Lucky for Mitch the Tennessee Bureau of Investigations was close by and had
responded in record time.

"Will do." Dixon stroked his forehead as if a headache had begun there. "One more thing, Sheriff. Chief
Lowden said he wouldn't push jurisdiction since Saylor
was one of ours. But he wants to be certain that we
keep him informed."

Mitch nodded. "I'll give him a call. Thanks,
Dixon."

Saylor was new on the force. His wife still lived in
Knoxville, waiting for their house to sell. There was a
call Mitch wasn't looking forward to making. But it

had to be done. He might as well go straight to the office and do it now. Chief Lowden had already broken the news to Mrs. Saylor in person. Mitch would have preferred to have done so himself, but that hadn't been possible. At this point he needed to intrude as little as possible.

"Let's go, Ashton."

His hands buried in his pockets, Ashton followed Mitch into the corridor. Mitch nodded to the deputy stationed outside the door, his thoughts going immediately back to the man trailing close behind him. Mitch imagined that fancy designer suit Ashton was wearing probably cost the equivalent of a full month's salary for a county sheriff. In spite of his expensive attire, Ashton seemed like a decent guy. He'd been amicable during the flight, filling Mitch in on what he knew of the case Alex was working, which wasn't a whole lot.

The involvement of the Bukovak name had proven a surprise to Mitch. Alex had apparently been looking into the disappearance of Marija Bukovak, a foreign exchange student from Croatia who had lived with Phillip and Nadine Malloy during the last school year. She'd left Tennessee more than three months ago to join her older sister in Chicago. But Marija never showed, and she hadn't been seen since the Malloys left her at the Nashville airport.

According to Ashton, the sister, Jasna, had given up trying to find Marija herself and had gone to the Colby Agency for help when the police failed to come up with any real answers. Mitch opted not to take offense at that remark. Jasna Bukovak had left a few things out when she'd told the Colby Agency her side of the story, but now wasn't the time to dwell on that. He wondered though why Alex hadn't just told him the truth about what she was doing in Shady Grove. It would certainly have made life simpler for him and her. But then, the truth would only have lent credence to what he'd already decided Alex was really up to—digging for dirt.

Mitch produced a smile for the duty nurse as he passed her station, then paused at the bank of elevators and stabbed the call button. A dozen questions whirled in his head, interfering with his ability to concentrate. Who in the world would have benefited from Miller's death? The man didn't have any money other than his deputy's salary. Everybody liked him. He was single and fairly popular with the women...which could possibly explain the reason he and Alex had been together.

An unfamiliar sensation joined the ballet of fragmented thoughts and feelings inside Mitch. His mouth drew into a frown. What the heck was that all about? First he had Ashton pegged as her lover, and then Mitch had moved on to scenarios with Miller. Mitch blew out a weary breath. He was too tired to think straight that's all. Too punchy to get a grip. He had to keep telling himself that a few hours shared over dinner that one night didn't change anything. He didn't know Alex Preston. She'd lied to him from the beginning.

A chime announced the imminent opening of the doors on the center elevator. Allowing Ashton to board first, Mitch stepped inside and depressed the lobby button. After he made the call to Saylor's wife, he'd need to check with the search commander and select the area that needed his and Ashton's support the most. Everything else on today's agenda could wait.

"Sheriff!"

Mitch held the door for Dixon who was double-timing down the corridor to join them. "One more thing," he said, a bit out of breath as he sidled into the waiting car. The doors closed behind him and the elevator slid into motion. "Roy's a little miffed that Willis wouldn't let him check the Preston woman's room over at the hotel. Willis didn't want to go in there without your authorization since it's still taped off."

Mitch grimaced at the thought of his overzealous cousin. Roy wanted to be the boss around the other men, but he knew Mitch wouldn't back him up if he overstepped his bounds, so he whined. Which only served to lessen his already poor popularity.

"Giving that room another look-see wouldn't hurt," Mitch allowed. "I think it was gone through pretty thoroughly the last time, but we might as well cover every base."

Dixon smiled. "I'll tell Roy he can do it personally."

Mitch resisted the urge to ask Dixon to do it himself. Roy would gloat over this triumph for weeks. That concern was quickly replaced as the memory of going through Alex's room that first time reeled through Mitch's mind. Touching her things. Feeling angry when one of his men commented on silky panties and hating himself for it. The stab of betrayal had pierced deep into his chest when faced with the reality of just how badly he'd been fooled by Alex Preston.

The elevator glided to a stop on the requested level and Mitch forced the haunting memories away. He glanced at Ashton, who had been particularly quiet for a lawyer. A wise man knows when to listen, Mitch decided as the three crossed the lobby. Ashton was likely building a case right now, and closely observing who he would consider his enemy. But Mitch wasn't his enemy, he only wanted to know who'd killed two of his deputies. And why. Murders just didn't happen in his county.

Still, he couldn't shake the feeling that there was more to Ashton's relationship with Alex than simply sharing the same employer. But that wasn't supposed to matter to Mitch since it had no apparent bearing on the case. Still, it did.

As Dixon drove away in a brown-and-tan cruiser, Mitch slid behind the wheel of his Jeep Wrangler. Ashton settled into the passenger side. Renewed dread pooled in Mitch's gut as he considered what he had to do first. He definitely was not looking forward to making that call. Saylor had been young. He and his wife had only been married for a couple of years. This whole thing was crazy. Mitch had himself two dead deputies in the space of just over twenty-four hours. To his knowledge, Raleigh County had never before lost a deputy in the line of duty.

"It's my thinking," Ashton said, breaking his lengthy silence, "that this incident should clear Alex of the murder charge." He said it as offhandedly as if he'd just commented on the nice weather they were having, but Mitch heard the tension hiding beneath that polished surface.

Oh yeah, the lawyer had been doing some serious thinking. Mitch backed out of the parking space, his gaze drifting up to the second-story window of the hospital room where Saylor had taken his last breath. "Maybe, maybe not," Mitch returned noncommittally.

"Come on, Sheriff," Ashton argued impatiently. "Do you think Alex shot at herself? She's running for her life. Someone tried to kill her. Maybe the same person who killed Miller. The shooter probably thinks she knows something or can identify him."

Mitch glanced first right then left before pulling out onto Commerce Street. That was one possibility. "Or maybe it was a setup by her accomplice to make her look innocent," he suggested, bracing for the other man's fury.

"What accomplice?" Ashton was more than a little annoyed now. "She came down here alone."

"So you say."

"Look, Hayden," Ashton snapped, dropping the title and any respect he'd so politely displayed before. "I've told you everything I know about the case Alex was working on, but I get the feeling that you're not being completely up-front with me. There's something you're leaving out."

Mitch braked at a red light and turned his attention fully to Ashton, who iced him down with one of those legal-eagle stares. Mitch supposed he should tell Ashton the rest. He'd know soon enough anyway...well, assuming they found Alex alive. Mitch refused to even consider the alternative.

"Her prints are on the murder weapon," he said finally.

Ashton shrugged. "And I'll bet Miller's are on his pistol. We have the proverbial standoff. Who shot first?"

Mitch mulled that one over for a while before responding. There was just too much he didn't understand, and a strong possibility existed that he might never know any more than he did right now, especially considering the circumstances. "That's the sixty-four thousand dollar question," he said in answer to Ashton's rhetorical jab. "There's no way to know which weapon fired first."

"What does Alex say happened?" he demanded.

"You've certainly avoided that question cleanly enough this morning."

"She doesn't know what happened," Mitch admitted, grinding out the words as he parked in his designated slot in front of the Raleigh County Sheriff's Department.

"What do you mean she doesn't know what happened?" Ashton asked warily.

Mitch withdrew his keys from the ignition and faced him. "She has retrograde amnesia. She doesn't remember anything since arriving in town."

Fury and something else less definitive etched itself across Ashton's features. "You said she was fine."

"She is fine. The gunshot didn't leave much more than a nasty flesh wound. The neurologist thinks the problem occurred when the back of her head slammed pretty hard into something, giving her a concussion. The scrapes and bruises she sustained indicate there was a struggle." Mitch shook his head, frowning with the same frustration that had plagued him for more than twenty-four hours. "We just don't know when or why. There was no indication that Miller had been involved in a struggle."

"So what are you saying," Ashton pressed, "that she can't remember *anything?*"

Mitch shook his head again. He wasn't sure he completely understood this himself. "She remembers everything prior to this case. She knows who she is, where she works—" he shrugged "—*everything,* except what I need her to."

"Victoria will want to call in a specialist."

"I already have." Mitch climbed out of his Jeep and rounded the hood. After waiting for Ashton to catch up, Mitch led the way to the building he called home the better part of every day. "He said she could remember some of it, all of it, or none of it." He paused at the door, leveling a gaze on the other man that he hoped conveyed the utter desperation of the situation. "Maybe today, maybe tomorrow, maybe never. And whatever she remembers will likely come in bits and pieces."

Ashton met that gaze with steel in his own. "So you've got no witnesses and no known motivation." He inclined his head in a gesture of triumph. "You've got no case, Sheriff. You can't even legally hold Alex any longer than you already have."

Ire knotted in Mitch's gut. "I'll tell you what I've got, Ashton," he said calmly, but a threatening quality belied his attempt at an even tone. "I've got her prints on the murder weapon and powder residue on her right hand. It may not be much, but it's all I'll need to build a case and you know it."

A slow grin slid across Ashton's face. "We'll just see about that, Hayden. There's no way Alex killed your deputy unless it was in self-defense. You'll never make me believe it, and you damn sure won't prove it in a court of law."

Mitch jerked the door open and went inside, Ashton came in behind him. That was the thing Mitch hated most about lawyers. They were always so sure of themselves. The urge to kick something surged through his veins. Too bad this lawyer was probably right. Not only would Mitch have a hell of a time making a charge stick under the circumstances, he was having entirely too much trouble believing it himself.

AFTER DROPPING Ashton at the only hotel in town, the same one where Alex had stayed when she first arrived in Shady Grove and the one now suspected as having been used by the shooter, Mitch drove home. He parked in front of his house and cut the engine. He stared for a long while at the dark structure. He rarely made it home at a decent hour anymore. And even when he got home, there was more work to be done.

God, he was bone-tired. Too tired to worry about opening the garage or putting the Jeep's rag top in place. Good thing there wasn't any rain in tonight's forecast. He leaned his head back against the headrest and closed his eyes for a minute. They'd turned over every rock in a ten-mile radius and found nothing. The APB hadn't garnered any information either. Alex had disappeared, just like the shooter who'd taken Saylor's life.

A weary burst of air hissed past Mitch's lips. Mrs. Saylor wanted her husband's body returned to Knoxville. Her father had passed along the instructions since she was in no condition to think much less talk or make decisions. Mitch had one of his men making the necessary arrangements. Then, at three o'clock that afternoon, the whole county had stopped everything to attend the memorial service for Deputy Miller. Just another low point in a particularly crappy day.

There hadn't been a murder in this county in over twenty years. Most criminals in the area seemed to prefer to do their dirty business in nearby Davidson or Rutherford Counties, specifically in the vicinity of Nashville. What the hell had Preston and Miller gotten involved in? Alex had only been in town a few days. How could one city girl wreak this much havoc in such a short time? Mitch refused to consider how much upset she'd generated for him personally in just a few hours. And where the hell had the drugs come from?

Miller was no user. And Mitch felt fairly confident that Alex wasn't either.

But then the only thing Mitch had known about Alex was that she was going around town asking questions about a good man who deserved better than to have some P.I. digging around in his private life. She hadn't mentioned the missing Bukovak girl as far as he knew. The best he could tell, she seemed to have been on some sort of mission to dig up dirt on Phillip Malloy, which could explain the drugs. Mitch had assumed that Phillip's opponent in the upcoming senatorial race had hired her to find some mud-slinging ammunition.

Mitch opened his eyes and forced away the guilt that instantly swamped him. The idea that she'd fooled him so thoroughly the first time they met that night at the diner had made him see red. He'd put a gag order of sorts into effect as soon as he found out what she was doing. In a small town like Shady Grove if the sheriff didn't want people talking about something, people didn't. When no one would answer the first question for her, she'd shown up at Mitch's door demanding that he stop interfering with her investigation. They'd argued, long and loud.

And the next morning, she'd been found…along with Miller.

Mitch slowly climbed out of his Jeep and walked even slower to his front door. He was tired and hungry, but worst of all he was disgusted. His emotions ran the gamut from fear for Alex's safety to anger that she'd escaped before he got the truth out of her, and that somehow she'd had something to do with all this. And then there was the other thing. The need that burned low in his belly. A need for her. The one that had started the moment they met. Even his fury at discovering she'd lied to him hadn't quenched that building fire. It was the craziest thing he'd ever experienced. He just couldn't shake it.

He cursed himself for his lack of self-control. Those amber eyes and full, lush lips haunted him still. The way her dark hair fell around her shoulders, enhancing her porcelain skin. He hadn't been able to keep his mind off her for long. Even now, as much as he wanted to know what had happened in the dark of night on that deserted road, some tiny part of him was glad that she didn't remember the last words he'd spoken to her.

If you don't stop nosing around my county, you'll be sorry.

Mitch grimaced at the memory. He'd been madder than hell. He'd known better than to let his temper get the better of him like that, but he supposed the bottom line had amounted to a mixture of fury and attraction. A dangerous combination under any circumstances.

He twisted the knob on his front door with a vengeance, and shoved it inward. There was no excuse for it. He'd acted like a fool. Stepping inside, he flipped the switch and flooded the long entry hall with light. He closed the door behind him and released a sigh of relief. In spite of the hellish day he'd had, and the still missing woman who made him seriously restless, he was glad to be home. It was late and he was spent. Things would have to look better in the morning.

Tossing his keys onto a nearby table, Mitch made his way down the hall toward his bedroom, shucking off his boots en route. Hopping on one foot and then the other, he peeled off his socks and tossed them aside. Fingers clumsy with exhaustion plucked at his buttons until he'd managed to undo the last one and pull his shirt from his waistband. As he reached his room, he started to shrug off his shoulder holster, but hesitated when a barely audible sound touched his ears.

He froze.

It came again…a whispered sigh or soft moan.

He cocked his head and listened intently as he slipped his weapon from its holster. His bare feet moved silently over the uncarpeted hardwood floor, instinctively avoiding the areas that creaked with age.

The word *no,* heavy with fear and denial, echoed…the disembodied voice closer this time. He paused at the door to his living room and listened again. Pure anguish, low and agonizing, reached out to him from the darkness with the next muffled sound. His heart beat faster as he leveled his weapon in that direction. Mitch eased into the room and hit the light switch. A pool of pale yellow glowed from a table lamp at the end of his sofa. His gaze moved beyond the table and the arm of the sofa to…

Alex.

Instantly, a shoulderload of Mitch's tension lifted. He reholstered his weapon. She lay on the old plaid sofa, tossing and turning, fighting some unseen demon in her sleep. The hospital gown and lab coat she wore over it had worked up her thighs, exposing long, shapely legs.

Moving closer, Mitch listened intently to make out her mumbled words but couldn't. Should he wake her? Maybe her dreams would help her remember. She whimpered in fear, and, unable to restrain himself, he crouched next to the sofa and shook her gently. She woke instantly, jerking upright and throwing her hands out in front of her in a defensive maneuver.

"Just take it easy," he soothed, clasping her forearms to keep her seated.

Her face was pale and her hair was mussed. The white bandage on her forehead stood out in stark relief against the dark tresses. She trembled visibly beneath his scrutiny. "It's okay," he assured her again. He noticed then that her knees were badly scraped—something new added to her list of injuries. But it was the fear and confusion in her eyes that made his gut clench.

"I didn't know where else to go," she told him, her voice shaky. She drew in a sharp breath as if suddenly remembering something she'd rather not. "I tried to stop him, but it was too late." She closed her eyes. "There was nothing I could do."

"I need to get you back to the hospital," Mitch suggested, fighting the urge to hold her.

Definitely the wrong thing to say.

With a good deal more strength than he would have imagined her capable, she shot to her feet, he came up with her.

"Don't take me back there. He'll find me!" She shook her head, her eyes wide with renewed fear. "He'll kill me!"

Mitch tightened his hold on her when she tried to pull away. "All right, we'll stay here for the time being. Just calm down." He wanted to ask who *he* was, but opted to do that later. "You need to relax."

She nodded stiffly. "As long as you promise you won't take me back there." Her expression clouded with too many emotions to read.

Blood, Saylor's blood, was smeared on the front of her gown and dried on her hands. She began to shake so hard that Mitch could no longer deny his need, he pulled her closer, to somehow comfort her…even when he knew he shouldn't.

"It's all right." He patted her back as she started to

cry softly against his chest. Her damp cheek felt warm against his bare skin. His arms tightened around her of their own volition, and Mitch closed his eyes in a futile attempt to ignore the mistake he was making.

He wasn't sure how long he stood that way, holding her close and whispering soothing sounds in her ear, but eventually reality dragged him to his senses.

Alex Preston was a suspect and the only witness he had to a murder, making this behavior completely unprofessional. He'd already been fooled once.

Mitch drew back, prying the clinging woman from his chest in the process. Her arms folded around her waist, hugging herself as her body quaked uncontrollably. He doubted she'd eaten anything all day. He had to get her comfortable and evaluate her condition further before he could question her. And then he'd have to call Ashton, but Mitch had every intention of putting that off for as long as possible.

"I'll tell you what, let's get you cleaned up and find something to eat. Then we'll straighten all this out. What do you say?"

She swiped at her eyes with the backs of her hands and nodded weakly. "Thank you."

He clenched his jaw against the protective feelings surging inside him. He couldn't say she was welcome. Hell, he shouldn't be doing this. Mitch took her by the arm and led her to the hall bathroom. "Wash your hands and face," he instructed, "and I'll get you some clothes."

She obeyed without question. She definitely wasn't herself. He might not know her well, but he knew that much. The Alex Preston he'd argued with was strong and self-reliant, not the submissive type at all.

Mitch hurried to his room and rounded up a T-shirt

and a pair of running shorts that tied at the waist. Right now wasn't the time to analyze why he hadn't already called in and reported finding her to the dispatcher, or the reason she'd chosen his house in which to take refuge. Chief Lowden would be annoyed that Mitch hadn't called him right away. But he had questions for Alex first. Questions that couldn't wait.

At least that was what he kept telling himself to justify putting off what he knew he should do. He paused outside the bathroom door. "This is the best I could do." He offered Alex the clothes. "There's a tube of antibiotic cream in the medicine cabinet for your knees."

Her hands not shaking quite so badly now, she accepted the items and managed a faint smile. "Thank you. This hospital getup is the pits." She shrugged out of the lab coat and dropped it to the floor. The back of the gown had worked its way open and was showing off more than she realized.

Mitch couldn't prevent the wicked grin that tilted his lips, or the equally wicked retort that flew out of his mouth before he could stop it. "I don't know, from some angles it's not so bad."

Realizing where he was looking she blushed and closed the door in his face. He shook his head in disbelief. He'd just flirted with her. What was wrong with him? Hadn't he learned his lesson already? Time for more coffee. Strong coffee. Because he definitely needed to clear his head.

By the time Alex found her way to the kitchen, the smell of fresh-brewed coffee had filled the air and Mitch had downed one cup and was working on a second.

"Have a seat." He motioned to the table and chairs

occupying the center of the big, old-fashioned kitchen. He reminded himself that he wasn't supposed to notice the athletic muscle tone of her legs, or the way his too-big T-shirt made her look even more vulnerable. "Coffee?"

"Please." She sat down gingerly.

He imagined that she was pretty sore from the unexplained beating she had taken. At least she wasn't shaking now, he noticed. He poured her a cup and sat it down on the table in front of her. "Are you hungry?"

She shook her head, then moistened her lips. Mitch cursed himself for following that last move with too much interest.

"I don't think I could handle any food right now."

She closed her eyes and he knew she was reliving the scene that had taken place in her hospital room.

"Why don't you tell me what happened."

Her eyes opened and she looked up at him with a kind of pain that tugged hard at his emotions. "I'd been lying there for what felt like forever trying to remember what went down with…with Deputy Miller." She shrugged halfheartedly. "Finally, I had to get up. I couldn't lie there a minute longer." Hesitating briefly, she frowned. "When I sat up I heard a sound like glass cracking and something hit the pillow right behind me. I guess it was instinct, but I rolled off the bed and onto the floor even before I realized what had actually happened. I knocked the telephone off the table in the process."

She stared into her cup for a while as she gathered her courage and began again. "I guess the deputy heard the crash. The door flew open and he rushed in. I tried to warn him to get down, but it happened too fast." She pressed trembling fingers to her mouth. "I tried to stop the bleeding…but I couldn't.'' Tears welled past her lashes and slid down her cheeks. "All I could think to do then was run from the danger."

"So you came here?" He worked hard not to be affected by her vulnerability, and at the same time to keep an open mind.

She nodded. "I was afraid. I didn't know where else to hide. I knew no one would look for me here. And this was the only other place I remembered besides the hotel."

She was right about that first part. No one would have ever looked here. Not even him. She obviously didn't remember the words that had passed between them in this very room on the night before last, since she felt comfortable coming here. "How can I be sure that you didn't call out to Deputy Saylor for the shooter to take down so that you could escape?"

"What?" She pushed out of her chair, sending it scraping across the floor. "Someone tried to kill me!"

Mitch sat his cup down, watching closely for every nuance of her reaction. He had to play devil's advocate. Had to see and feel her response. "The second bullet could have been the one that hit your pillow to make it look as if someone was trying to kill you."

She braced her hands at her waist. "You can't believe that. Why would I have come here? Why would I try to help that deputy if I'd wanted him dead? Do you think I would have—?" A gasp stole the rest of what she intended to say as her mind evidently replayed those final moments in the hospital.

"I'm sorry, Ms. Preston," Mitch offered, with absolutely no contrition. "But until we solve this case, you're my prime suspect. Despite the fact that you came here, running only made you look more guilty."

She stared directly into his eyes. "I ran because I was afraid. I don't know why I came to your house," she said flatly. "And I can't tell you what happened in that car with Miller." She flung her arms upward in frustration. "I don't even know how I got all these bruises. But the one thing I can tell you is that I didn't kill anyone. *I know that.*"

She swayed slightly and had the presence of mind to drop back into her chair before Mitch had to reach for her.

"All right," he relented. "Let's say for the moment that I believe you. How do you propose we go about proving your story? After all, you lied to me about why you were here from the beginning." She might not remember just yet, but he couldn't put it out of his head.

That got her attention. Confusion claimed her features. "I don't know why I lied to you. But there must have been a reason I held anything back."

Incredibly, he believed her. Mitch swore silently. This was nuts. He should just take her back to the hospital this minute and put her under guard in a room with no windows. What the hell was he thinking standing here allowing himself to swallow her story hook, line and sinker?

But he did. That was the hell of it. He was furious that the Colby Agency had sent her here without coordinating with his office. He was even angrier that she had lied to him and that she seemed determined to make Phillip look bad somehow. But, damned if he didn't believe, deep in his gut, that she was innocent of any wrongdoing where the murders were concerned.

Before he opened his mouth and made an even bigger fool of himself, the telephone rang. He crossed the room and snatched up the receiver before the second ring. "Hayden."

"Sheriff, you're not going to believe what me and Willis found in that P.I.'s hotel room."

It was Roy. Mitch glanced at the clock. "Roy, I thought everyone had called it a night?"

"I know," he crooned. "But I just couldn't wait till morning to do this. I talked Willis into coming over here with me after the search ended for the night."

Mitch studied Alex, who was staring into her coffee cup again as if it held all the answers she needed. "So what'd you find?"

Roy's excitement was palpable. "We found a high-powered rifle hidden under the mattress. How much you want to bet it's the same one that killed Saylor?"

Chapter Two

Mitch sat in the darkness of his bedroom staring at the telephone on the table next to the bed. A faint beam from the moon filtered through the curtains silhouetting the table and the items that sat upon it. The digital alarm clock read 12:45 a.m.

He leaned back in his chair and told himself again that he couldn't delay making that call any longer. For almost an hour now he'd been sitting here like this, mulling over all that had happened and putting off the inevitable. Roy had called his buddy in ballistics and gotten the promise of a priority test to confirm if the high-powered rifle found in Alex's hotel room was, in fact, the one used to kill Saylor. They would have their answer some time tomorrow.

Mitch hadn't told Roy that he had Alex in custody. What was the point? The search wouldn't resume until daybreak. That was soon enough to announce the news in Mitch's opinion, though for the life of him he couldn't understand why he was delaying that call as well. He told himself that it was the right thing to do. First he needed to interrogate Alex further, and he wanted to do that on his own terms.

She wasn't up to questioning tonight, that was certain. He hadn't bothered to tell her about the rifle they'd found either. She might make a run for it in the middle of the night if she thought that new evidence, which made her look even guiltier, had been found. Continuing to behave in a completely unprofessional manner, Mitch had allowed her to finish her coffee and then he'd shown her to his spare room. Fifteen minutes later she'd been sleeping like a baby.

Opting to keep her whereabouts to himself until morning might not really bother anyone connected with the official search, but not telling Ashton was a whole other can of worms. There would be hell to pay if he didn't tell Ashton. Whatever the man's personal claim on Alex, as her attorney he wouldn't appreciate being made to wait a moment longer than necessary.

Pushing to his feet, Mitch blew out a weary breath. He padded across the carpeted floor and sat down on the edge of his unmade bed. Until just over one week ago his professional life had been pretty much a breeze, other than the long hours. The worse thing that ever happened was the occasional drunken brawl at one of the college hangouts, or, even more infrequently, at the campus itself. With its five thousand students, Fulmer College was a pretty busy place. Despite the number of rowdy college students the school seemed to draw, trouble rarely found its way into Raleigh County.

But it sure as hell had waltzed into town with Alex Preston. She'd managed to not only turn his professional world upside down, but his personal life as well.

After calling information and requesting the number for the hotel, Mitch selected the option so the number would be automatically dialed. His voice rusty with sleep, the desk clerk offered his practiced welcome greeting, then transferred the call to Ashton's room.

He answered on the first ring.

So, Mitch wasn't the only one who couldn't sleep. The thought only irritated him all the more. "This is Hayden. I've found Alex."

"Is she all right?"

As had been the case from the start, the anticipation in the other man's voice was a good deal more than professional concern. His relationship with Alex clearly went much deeper. That shouldn't bother Mitch, but somehow it did.

"She's fine."

"And what does that mean?" Ashton snapped. "The last time you told me she was fine, she'd lost part of her memory. Where is she?"

Mitch struggled to control the unwarranted fury that rocketed inside him. "I said she's fine. She's sleeping."

"Where the hell is she?"

"Here," Mitch ground out. "At my house."

The brief silence on the other end of the line spoke volumes. "Why is she at your house?" Ashton's tone was guarded this time, almost accusing.

"She said she figured it was the last place anyone would look." Mitch massaged his stubbled jaw in an attempt to stop the muscle jerking there.

"Give me directions," Ashton ordered, "I'll be right there."

"No. I told you she's sleeping."

More silence.

"You can see her in the morning," Mitch offered.

"I don't know what you think you're up to Hayden, but you'd better think long and hard before you step too far over that line. I won't tolerate you coming between me and my client."

Mitch shrugged off his shoulder holster and tossed it onto the bed behind him. ''I'm getting tired of your threats, Ashton.'' He gritted his teeth to hold back the rest of what he wanted to say. This was Mitch's county. He didn't need any big-city know-it-all telling him how to take care of his business.

''You can't stop me from seeing her, you know that.''

''I have no intention of trying to stop you,'' Mitch pointed out. ''Be at my office at nine in the morning. You can see her then.''

That tense silence again. ''I'll be there at eight,'' Ashton countered hotly, ''and if you ask her just one question outside my presence I swear you'll regret it.''

''I wouldn't dream of questioning her without you,'' Mitch assured him. ''See you at nine.'' He hung up the receiver before Ashton could protest.

One thing was crystal clear, Mitch decided as he climbed into bed with his usual sleeping companion, his weapon, he had to get his head together before morning. Whatever it was that had allowed Alex to get so deeply under his skin in such a short time, he had to find a way to ignore it. Because if Mitch was half as easy to read where Alex was concerned as Ashton was, the hotshot lawyer already knew too much.

ALEX SLOWLY OPENED her eyes and stared at the ceiling of her room. Something was different, but she couldn't be sure what. A dull ache throbbed deep in her skull, making focused concentration impossible. She stretched and sore muscles screamed in protest. The memory of a fist slamming into her stomach, of steel fingers gripping her throat and shoving her hard ricocheted through her mind. The ache in her skull exploded into fierce pain. She groaned and sat up, resting her head in her hands.

It took her a few seconds to realize the fierce agony wasn't real, only remembered from an event that hovered behind an impenetrable wall that wouldn't allow her to recall the last six days of her life. When she'd finally convinced herself it wasn't real, the dull ache was all that remained.

How had she lost that whole block of time? Why couldn't she remember? The concept seemed completely foreign to her. She should simply be able to retrieve those lost hours like so much data on a floppy disk. But she couldn't. The flash of memory she'd just experienced was only the second little frame of recall she'd had since waking up in the hospital the day before yesterday.

The neurologist had said that it could be all or nothing, and would likely come in spurts. There was no way to speculate how much she would recall, and no reliable means to speed up her recovery.

Frowning, Alex returned to the problem at hand. Where was she? The image of Mitch Hayden offering her clean clothes at the bathroom door zoomed into vivid 3-D focus. She was at his house. That's right. She'd come here because she knew no one would look for her here...she'd be safe. Something else she couldn't remember nagged at her, making her a little less sure of the safe part, but she couldn't grasp it. She hadn't actually left the hospital with this destination in mind, she'd just wound up here and then the notion that no one would look for her at this particular location had gelled. He was the sheriff, after all, why would anyone look for her at his house?

Gingerly, she touched the bandage on her forehead.

The image of fire blasting from the muzzle of a hand-gun aimed at her face seized her. She gasped with re-membered terror and hugged her arms around her mid-dle. She squeezed her eyes shut and rocked back and forth to calm herself. Her heart pounded so hard her chest hurt. *He* was going to kill her. *He* would never let her live knowing what she surely knew—his iden-tity. Alex didn't know how she knew it was a he, she just did. She was as certain of it as she was that he would try to kill her before she remembered. He had to...

"Good morning."

Alex snapped her eyes open at the sound of a deep male voice. Mitch Hayden's slow southern drawl to be exact. He stood in the doorway, propped against the frame. As she watched, he straightened and moved to-ward the bed. She grappled for the composure that usu-ally came so easily for her. Whoever had worked her over had definitely scrambled her thinking. She was in the middle of a huge identity crisis that involved mur-der and mayhem and all she could do at the moment was notice how good the sheriff looked. Flashes of memory from last night kept popping into her head. His shirt hanging open, revealing a magnificent chest. His scent, something male and musky, when he'd held her so close as she broke down in his arms. Something about him drew her. It didn't make sense.

"Good morning," she returned as calmly as her churning emotions would allow when he paused a few feet away. Feeling vulnerable in her current position, she climbed out of bed and straightened her borrowed clothes, then combed her fingers through her hair in an attempt to pull herself together on the outside at least.

"I appreciate you not taking me back to the hospital last night."

"You don't need to thank me," he said quietly, those Artic-blue eyes clocking her every move. "It wasn't a favor to you. I had my reasons."

She was his prime suspect. How could she forget? Alex folded her arms over her chest and for a long moment studied the handsome sheriff who appeared hell-bent on adding to her misery. One single frame of memory flickered—Mitch Hayden angry and shouting at her. She flinched. The snatch of recall disintegrated as suddenly as it appeared. She cursed silently for not being able to hold on to the fleeting images long enough to decipher what they meant. She had to remember. Her freedom—not to mention her life—depended upon it.

"I didn't shoot either of those men." Alex blinked back the uncharacteristic urge to cry. She was stronger than this. She straightened her shoulders and lifted her chin. Much stronger. "In fact, I think you should stop wasting time trying to decide whether or not I'm guilty."

He lifted one tawny eyebrow. "What makes you think I haven't already decided?"

Uncertainty pulled the plug on her bravado, but she stood firm against the sinking feeling. "If you had, I'd have been in a cell this morning instead of in your bed."

That cool gaze flicked from her to the rumpled sheets and back. "This isn't *my* bed," he said tightly.

Drawing courage from her direct hit, she replied, "Close enough."

Quite obviously ill at ease now, he turned back toward the door and started out of the room. "You should eat. You're going to need your strength. I'll wait for you in the kitchen.''

Was that a warning? Alex mused as she watched him go. It sure sounded like one. She frowned when she considered that she needed to call Victoria. That first day in the hospital she'd been too disoriented to call anyone, then the killer had struck again before she'd had a chance to demand her rights be acknowledged. Alex squeezed her eyes shut to block the vivid mental images that accompanied the memory of Deputy Saylor's murder.

Determined to pull it together she headed in the direction of the bathroom she'd used last night. She had to find a way to clear herself of suspicion. And since her memory was not cooperating, she'd just have to utilize her investigative skills.

Alex closed and locked the bathroom door, then took care of essentials. As she washed her hands she studied her reflection in the mirror. Her right cheek was still slightly discolored from...the sound of the back of a hand slapping against her cheek reverberated in her head. She jerked at the remembered sting. Alex touched her cheek and tried to remember more. Trees. Darkness. Someone shouting in the background. A male voice. The feel of the leaf-covered ground beneath her. The wind going out of her lungs when someone kicked her in the stomach. The sound of gunfire. Stark fear.

Trembling violently, she snapped back to the here and now. Alex fumbled around in the drawers until she found a brush. Taking slow, deep breaths to counter the adrenaline surging inside her body, she tugged the brush through her hair. Calm down, she ordered the frightened eyes in the mirror. *You're safe now.* Sheriff

Hayden had no intention of allowing anything to happen to her. She was his only witness—and suspect. Another of those fleeting images slipped in then out of her thoughts. Hayden shouting at her, fury in his expression. And then that strong pull she felt for him…some kind of unexplainable connection.

Alex shook off the worrisome thoughts and forced one foot in front of the other until she found him in the kitchen. He'd poured her a cup of coffee and prepared toast. He stood, leaning against a nearby counter, waiting patiently.

He wanted answers. The evidence against her was apparently considerable since he wasn't out beating the bushes for another suspect. Or maybe he just hoped she would remember everything and save him the trouble. She sat down and took a much-needed sip of coffee. Her stomach rumbled. She tasted the toast he had gone to the trouble to butter and waited for him to begin his new round of interrogation.

But he didn't.

Unable to tolerate the prolonged anticipation, she asked, "How does the evidence stack up against me?"

"Your prints are on the murder weapon." He nodded to the right hand she'd just lifted to take another bite of toast. "You had the powder residue to prove you were holding the weapon when it fired."

Alex stared at her hand. She swallowed, hard. Her appetite vanished and she dropped the toast back onto the saucer. "Well, there's a good start for a murder case," she allowed. She stared directly at him then. "Now all you need is motive, and you can nail me."

She didn't miss the little flutter of muscle in his tightly clenched jaw before he responded. "That would help. But then, if I have to, I'll nail you without it if you killed my deputy.''

Averting her gaze from his intense one, she sipped her coffee thoughtfully. Anxiety coiled in her stomach threatening her flimsy hold on composure, chinking away at her certainty that she was innocent. She had to be. She would never kill anyone unless it was to save her own life—or someone else's. Some part of her felt like the sheriff knew it, too. Otherwise she would be in a cell.

''You realize, of course, that I don't have to answer any questions without legal counsel present,'' she said then. She hardly recognized the strained voice as her own. God, she was a mess.

''I didn't ask any questions.'' Those too-discerning eyes remained focused on hers.

Alex almost laughed at that one. He wouldn't ask any questions, because he knew that legally he couldn't. But he could make her feel the pressure of proving her innocence. ''I can't tell you what happened, because I don't know,'' she admitted with complete candor. ''And I don't know how Miller tied into my investigation, but he isn't the reason I came here.''

Hayden didn't say a word. He simply stood there, waiting for her to continue if she chose.

''I came to Shady Grove to look into the disappearance of Marija Bukovak, a foreign exchange student from Croatia.'' He didn't even blink. ''She was staying here with a local family, the Malloys. She hasn't been seen since they left her at the airport about three months ago. Jasna, her sister, didn't feel like the police had done enough so she asked my agency to see what we could find.''

A subtle change in his expression told her that her last remark didn't sit too well with him.

"Did she also tell you that there have been a series of murders in the Nashville and Murfreesboro areas that the police believe might be connected to her sister's disappearance?"

Her brow creased in confusion. There had been no mention of any kind of ongoing investigation connected to Marija's disappearance. "What murders?"

"The sophomore murders," he explained. "Six young women were found between April and July of this year, all students at nearby universities. Each was sexually assaulted, strangled to death and then buried in a shallow grave in the woods. The Tennessee Bureau of Investigations apprehended the killer last month. Davidson County thinks maybe the Bukovak girl was one of his victims, but he hasn't confessed to the crime. She's the only unsolved case of a missing person from this area that fits the profile."

"He confessed to having murdered the other six?"

Hayden eyed her speculatively for a couple of seconds before answering. "He did."

Alex shook her head. "Then he didn't do the Bukovak girl," she said succinctly.

He inclined his head and lifted a skeptical brow. "You're positive about that."

"Absolutely." She chewed on a bite of toast as she considered all that he'd told her, then washed it down with more coffee. "Serial killers don't work that way. If he confessed, he confessed all. He wouldn't have bothered otherwise." She frowned. "Unless he's playing some sort of game. He might reveal bits and pieces if that's the case."

"And you would be an expert in that area," he suggested, still looking skeptical.

"Yes." She pushed the remainder of her breakfast away. "Didn't the TBI guys come to the same conclusion?" If they hadn't, then they needed to be in another line of work.

"That was their feeling, but no one can really be sure." Hayden glanced at her half-eaten toast. "Are you finished?"

She stood. "I'd like to call Victoria Colby, she's my boss and I need to check in."

"I've already talked to Mrs. Colby." He pushed off from the counter. "Come on. We'll stop by your hotel room and pick up a change of clothes and some shoes."

Surprised, Alex stared after him as he left the room. "When did you call?" she asked, following him into the hall.

"I didn't. I flew up there to find out what you were working on." He stopped and turned to face her.

Alex was a little slower to react, almost running into him before she stopped. When her gaze connected with his she wasn't prepared for the rush of sensations that accompanied standing so close to him and looking directly into his eyes. Warmth spread through her middle, and her heart kicked into a faster rhythm.

"Your friend Ashton came back with me. He'll be meeting us at my office at nine."

"Zach is here?" A smile stretched across her face and a great deal of the weight sagging her shoulders lifted. She needed him right now. At least he would be on her side.

Something changed in the sheriff's eyes, but Alex couldn't quite read what she saw there. "He's here,"

Hayden affirmed. "We should get going so we don't keep him waiting."

MITCH WATCHED the reunion with growing irritation—mostly with himself. After the emotional embraces and assurances were exchanged, Ashton still managed to find a way to touch Alex. He squeezed her hand… touched her bruised cheek. Mitch hated that it disturbed him so, but it did just the same. He hated even more the curious glances his bringing Alex in had generated among his own men. The glare Ashton had arrowed at him the moment they stepped through the door had been blistering. Any one of those things should have made Mitch realize just how far out of bounds he'd allowed his judgment to go. But none did.

That one night at the diner he and Alex had somehow connected over the blue plate special. Hours of nothing but talking and laughing and too-intense eye contact. He just couldn't shake that strange bond now. The connection had been electric…still was. And it was playing havoc with his ability to look at this case objectively. Case in point, she'd been lying to him the whole time. Told him that she was just passing through. And he'd believed her. That almost-kiss when he'd walked her to her car that night still stirred his blood.

The very next morning he'd found out who she really was. He'd been furious with himself for being so gullible. It wasn't going to happen again. And look at him now. The only highlight of the whole mess was that she didn't seem to remember anything about that night either, and he'd just as soon it stayed that way. He didn't relish the idea of being recognized as a fool twice.

Mitch forced those thoughts away. "We should get

started,'' he announced, interrupting the hushed exchange taking place in the middle of his own office.

Ashton guided Alex to a visitor's chair, his hand at the small of her back, the gesture clearly welcome and familiar. Mitch gritted his teeth against how that simple move made him feel. He rationalized his unwarranted emotions with the fact that she was a suspect and a witness. Her well-being was supposed to be important to him and the case.

Good one, Hayden, he chastised silently.

Ashton took the seat next to her. "You broke the rules, Hayden," he accused, a new glare now directed at Mitch.

Mitch settled into his own chair. "I didn't ask her a single question."

When Ashton would have argued semantics, Alex raised a hand to stop him. "He didn't ask, Zach," she assured him. "I want this cleared up just as much as he does."

"I'm not sure you're up to this," Ashton argued.

"I'm fine." She sat straighter in her chair. "I just can't remember the things I need to."

Mitch studied her as she protested Ashton's attempts to sway her into being reevaluated by a specialist of his choosing. She could hold her own with the guy. And that only made her more appealing.

She'd twisted her shoulder-length hair up into a youthful but conservative style, showing off that long, slender neck. The navy slacks and pale blue blouse fit a little loosely. For comfort, Mitch supposed. Alex didn't strike him as the type who would forego comfort to show off her figure. Besides, he'd already seen enough of her to know she had a terrific body. His own body tightened at the remembered feel of hers when he'd held her.

He shut off that line of thinking and focused on the matter at hand. He had two dead deputies. And Alex Preston was somehow involved in their deaths, if by no other means than the fact that she was present at both shootings.

"Let's start by you telling me how you got out of the hospital and to my house," Mitch said, dragging the two from the heated discussion.

To his credit, Ashton kept his mouth shut.

Alex thought for a while before she spoke. Her expression grew solemn. "When I was sure I couldn't help the deputy, I made my way to the door and into the corridor. I was afraid that whoever was shooting at me would try again...." She frowned. "Or maybe come after me.

"Once I got into the corridor I considered going to the nurse's desk, but there wasn't anyone there. It was like everyone had disappeared. That spooked me. I started for the elevators, but one opened and I was afraid it was the shooter, so I hid behind the closest door, which turned out to be a supply closet."

"That's where you got the lab coat," Mitch guessed.

She nodded. "When the coast was clear I ran like hell. I don't think anyone even noticed I was missing from the room until after I'd left the hospital. The shots didn't make that much noise. I don't know if Saylor would even have heard anything if I hadn't bumped into the table and knocked the telephone off it." She blinked, her eyes bright.

The shooter had used a sound suppressor, which explained why no one at the hotel seemed to have heard anything. Both items were being tested by ballistics at that very moment.

"How did you get out of town," he prodded. That was the part that bothered him the most. She'd been barefoot and without transportation. Someone had to have given her a lift.

"The rug guy," she explained. "He had already taken the mats at the front of the hospital lobby entrance and gone back to his van for clean ones. While he put the new ones in place I hid in the back of his van." She shrugged. "When he made his next stop I got out. It was a nursing home outside town."

Pinecrest, but that was still a good five miles from Mitch's house. "You walked from there?"

She smiled dimly. "Walked, ran, stumbled. I've got a few blisters to prove it. Mostly I hid in the woods afraid someone would find me."

Mitch thought about her scraped knees, then about her hovering in the bushes. "When did you get to my house?"

She chewed her lower lip, thoughtful. "Sometime after dark. The door was unlocked so I went on inside."

"You didn't call anyone?"

She shook her head. "I couldn't think. I was exhausted. My head hurt. I just needed to lie down. I fell asleep on the couch and then you came in."

"And you've told me everything you can remember regarding what you discovered during the course of your investigation?" he pressed. He needed her to give him everything, no matter how unimportant it might seem. "You remember nothing as to why you were meeting with Miller?"

"I'm sorry, no. I don't even remember talking to

him at all. Like I said, my agency was hired to look into Marija's disappearance and the family she was staying with, the Malloys. I still plan to pursue that investigation.''

Mitch tapped the arm of his chair considering her words for a moment. "Even after I told you what the TBI believes, you want to move forward?''

She nodded. "Her sister's counting on me. I can't in good conscience walk away without giving it my best shot.'' She pursed those lush lips for a time. There was something about her mouth, the shape or color or maybe both, but he wanted to taste her so badly that it was an ache inside him.

"Besides,'' she continued, ''I'm not sure I can buy into the serial killer scenario considering Marija's circumstances and the Malloy connection.''

A new kind of dread rising, Mitch asked, "What circumstances?'' Marija had fit the serial killer's profile perfectly. Since she hadn't been found, that seemed the most likely scenario. Unless she just didn't want to be found.

"Jasna may not have shared this information with the police since it was so private,'' Alex began. ''But two days before Marija disappeared she called her sister and admitted that she was pregnant. Jasna felt certain that the father was Mr. Malloy since Marija was so afraid he'd find out. It's possible he discovered her pregnancy and decided he couldn't risk the bad publicity considering the upcoming senatorial race. Not to mention his wife's reaction.''

A chunk of ice formed in Mitch's gut. Shock radiated through him. "That's impossible,'' he said tightly.

"Why would my client lie?'' Alex countered.

"She has to be lying,'' Mitch returned, his tone brittle despite his best efforts to keep it even. "Phillip Malloy is one of the finest men I know." He leveled his gaze on hers. "And I should know, he's my uncle."

"So that automatically clears him of possible wrong-doing?" Ashton countered. "I don't think so."

Alex shot Ashton a quelling look. Mitch wanted to reach across his desk and wring the guy's neck. "If you can't prove that allegation, I would caution you to keep it to yourself."

"I'm not accusing him—"

"Is that a threat, sheriff?" Ashton cut Alex off, leaning forward in his chair. "Because if it is, you're making one hell of a big mistake."

"Zach," Alex warned, placing a hand on his arm.

Ashton shook off her restraining gesture and stood, glaring down at Mitch. "Make a formal charge, Hayden, or we're out of here."

Mitch smiled, the gesture filled with the contempt strumming through him. "If that's what you want."

"Zach, this is not the way to handle this." Alex was standing now, too. She pulled him around to face her. "Let me do my job. Okay? You're not helping," she added when he still looked skeptical. "I have to think about what's best for my client."

Ashton held up his hands, stop sign fashion. "Fine." He sent a glower in Mitch's direction. "He can't charge you anyway. He doesn't have enough evidence to make a case and he knows it."

Mitch leaned back in his chair, cocked his head and stared right back at Ashton. "I guess I forgot to mention the new evidence we discovered last night."

Alex's expression fell; Ashton's grew wary.

"What evidence?" he demanded with a little less conviction.

"A high-powered rifle, complete with sound suppressor, was found in the hotel room Alex used. It was hidden beneath the mattress."

She shook her head. "That can't be."

"It's a setup." Zach shook a finger in Mitch's direction. "And you know it."

Mitch stood. He pressed his palms against his desktop and leaned forward, his gaze never leaving Ashton's. "Maybe it is a setup. Alex certainly appears to have no motivation for whatever the hell is going on here. But that's beside the point. I have every intention of getting to the bottom of this one way or another." He turned his attention to Alex then. "I will have your full cooperation."

"Absolutely." Her gaze never wavered. "It's in my best interest as well as my client's."

Mitch shifted his focus back to Ashton. "And we'll do things *my* way."

Before Ashton could respond, the door to Mitch's office swung inward. Dixon stuck his head in. "Sorry to interrupt, Sheriff, Peg stepped out a minute. And you've got an urgent call on line two. It's Detective Wells from Davidson County."

Mitch snatched up the receiver as Dixon pulled the door closed behind him. "Hayden." Dammit. He didn't need any interruptions right now.

"Hey, Mitch. Wells here. You have an Alex Preston in protective custody in regards to the Miller case?"

"That's right." Mitch ignored the rapt attention focused on him from across the desk. What the hell was this about? Alex hadn't been out of his sight all night.

"We've got what looks like a suicide up here. We found a business card for Preston in the woman's room," Wells added. "I think maybe you'd better come have a look." He rattled off the location.

"What's the victim's name?" Mitch stiffened when he heard it. "I'll be there in half an hour." He dropped the receiver back into its cradle and settled his gaze on Alex's expectant one. "Your client no longer has an interest in this case, Ms. Preston."

"What are you saying?" Uncertainty flickered in her amber eyes.

"Jasna Bukovak is dead."

Chapter Three

Alex sat in Hayden's Jeep feeling more than a little numb. Jasna was dead. Alex blinked and refocused her attention on the passing suburban landscape. The leaves were turning colors already. Golds and russets were sprinkled amid the collage of greens. And though it was a month away, the occasional yard was decorated for fall's first major event. Bales of straw, pumpkins, black cats and an assortment of scarecrows.

Jasna Bukovak would never see another holiday with her sister, even if Alex could find the missing girl.

It was over.

Alex wracked her brain for any tidbit of conversation she'd had with Jasna since arriving in Raleigh County, but nothing came to mind. Surely she had not learned anything that would have banished all hope for the young woman. Alex refused to believe that. She would surely remember anything so life-altering. She sighed with resignation. Then again, maybe not.

She turned to the driver and considered what little she knew about the sheriff. Alex focused on the man behind that chiseled jaw and those cool blue eyes. He was highly regarded by his men. That had been obvious both this morning and during her stay in the hospital.

The deputies were immensely loyal. Alex hadn't found a complainer in the bunch. That said a lot about Mitch Hayden. If his men liked and respected him, then he was a fair man, a man of his word. His grief at the loss of two of his men was painfully clear. He wouldn't stop until he found the person responsible for their deaths.

Though he allowed her to believe that she was still his prime suspect, Alex felt fairly confident that he knew deep in his gut that she was innocent. He'd shown entirely too much leniency to maintain otherwise. She wondered how a man as young as Hayden, thirty maybe, had garnered himself such a highly respected reputation. She supposed he possessed more charm and political finesse than she'd seen so far. But then, according to the research she'd done before coming to Shady Grove, the Haydens had run this county for more than fifty years. That was likely the key factor more so than any of his assets, and he had many that had nothing at all to do with personality. She shivered at the thought of those strong arms around her.

For the most part, Alex was pretty sure she had him figured out. He was a straight shooter. Probably a little too righteous for some of his counterparts, but preferred by most. She doubted he had much of a social life outside recreational sex considering the hours he appeared to put in. The thought of sex with Mitch Hayden sent another shiver through her.

Alex shook off that ridiculous notion and forced her attention forward. Just because the man didn't wear a wedding ring or have an answering machine loaded with calls from prospective lovers didn't mean he ignored his natural instincts. He was too good-looking and in too public a position not to have his share of feminine attention.

None of which was her concern. Alex touched the bandage on her forehead. She had bigger problems than Mitch Hayden's sex life. Two men were dead, Jasna was dead, and somehow Alex was caught right smack in the middle of it. And she couldn't remember why or how. Not to mention that she'd stuck both feet into her mouth by mentioning Marija's possible pregnancy. If Alex had ever known that the Malloys were relatives of Hayden, she'd definitely forgotten that little tidbit. Getting any information on the family now would be next to impossible. Hayden would make sure of that.

She started when another of those high-speed flashes of memory zoomed through her head. Mitch Hayden yelling at her. Alex strained to recapture the images, but couldn't. If the memory was real, the handsome sheriff had been madder than hell about something.

How could one missing nineteen-year-old young woman have spawned this kind of chain reaction? What had Alex seen or heard that made her a liability?

Hayden slowed and turned left into the drive of a small two-story frame house. Several cars were already there. Some were Nashville P.D., others were unmarked. The house and its miniscule yard had been cordoned off with yellow crime-scene tape. Before Alex realized Hayden had emerged from the vehicle, he stood next to her waiting for her to get out. She dragged her attention from the well-maintained house to the man who'd brought her here. Those blue eyes were analyzing her closely now. Too closely.

"I've been here before," she said abruptly, uncertain where the knowledge came from. "I don't know when or why. I only know that I've been here."

Something changed in those assessing eyes, but she couldn't say just what. "You don't have to go inside," he offered with too much understanding.

Alex climbed out of the vehicle to stand between it and its owner. "Yes, I do," she replied, careful to keep her gaze on the house before her rather than the man standing so very close.

Zach had said the same thing. He hadn't wanted Alex to come. But she'd insisted. She'd also insisted that he didn't. He needed to bring Victoria up to speed and Alex didn't need him butting heads with Hayden. Zach had her best interest at heart, but she couldn't do her job with him hovering nearby. He still felt possessive of her when it came to her safety. Alex loved him for it, but his determination not to let anything happen to her could be irritating at times.

She was immensely thankful for his friendship. Their brief relationship hadn't changed how they felt about each other. It had only proven that they weren't suited for anything other than good friends.

"You're sure you're up to this?"

Startled out of her reverie, Alex turned to face the man who'd spoken. Heat instantly rushed through her, leaving her a little shaky and a lot uncertain of herself. She remembered those strong arms around her, the feel of his bare chest beneath her cheek. Whatever the attraction between her and this stranger, it was powerful and more than a little unsettling.

"We're wasting time, Sheriff. I need to do this."

He studied her a moment longer as if still doubtful of what exactly she hoped to accomplish. "All right," he relented, stepping back.

Hayden led the way to the front door of the small boarding house where Jasna had taken a room. She'd planned to stay in the vicinity until her sister was found. The uniformed officer standing guard at the front door stepped aside without question for them to pass. Inside a steady stream of personnel wearing their bureaucratic camouflage moved up and down the stairs and from room to room.

In the shared living room, a young man and two older women were being questioned. The other tenants, Alex supposed, and maybe the owner. The owner had started renting rooms to make ends meet after her husband died. She kept a clean house and prepared home-cooked meals, according to Jasna. She'd felt comfortable here. Startled that she suddenly knew so much about the place, Alex shivered. This was eerie. But a good sign, wasn't it? She needed to remember so much more.

"Mitch!" A man of about fifty and wearing a wrinkled tan suit called from the second-story landing. "Up here."

Alex followed Mitch up the stairs. Her chest felt too tight. Her stomach roiled. She took three long, deep breaths to counter the panic mushrooming inside her. This would by no means be the first dead body she'd viewed. She summoned the objectivity and nerves of steel she had developed over the years. This was not the time to fall apart. She'd barely convinced Hayden to allow her to participate in this investigation. She wasn't about to blow it now by puking or passing out.

Jasna's room looked exactly the way it had the one other time Alex had been there. Clean and uncluttered by personal possessions. Despite the lack of personal touches, the old iron bed and hand-stitched quilt gave the room a feeling of home. Alex studied the room carefully, taking in every detail and allowing the feel of it to wash over her.

"In here," the cop in the tan suit said, motioning toward another door.

Hayden stepped into the tiny bathroom first. Alex moved in beside him. The metallic smell of blood hit her instantly, her stomach clenched. More deep breaths. Alex felt the color drain from her face and she suddenly became cold.

Jasna lay in the empty tub, her life seeped out through the ugly slits in her wrists. She was naked save for the silver chain she always wore. Her sister wore one exactly like it. Both chains held half of a small silver heart. When placed side by side, the word *sisters* formed.

Alex closed her eyes and said a quick prayer for Jasna. And then added an extra word of supplication for Marija. Two young girls who'd already suffered too much loss in their lives and now this. Alex turned away and blinked back the burn of tears.

What evil had done this?

She would not believe that Jasna had taken her own life.

Mitch crouched next to the tub and surveyed Jasna Bukovak's body. He'd only met her once. She'd come to him regarding her sister and there hadn't been anything he could do but refer her to TBI after he'd spoken with Phillip and Nadine. There was no proof of foul play and Marija was old enough to have simply decided to disappear. Yet, Jasna had been convinced her sister had not done so of her own free will. And since she fit the serial killer's profile, that was a distinct possibility.

Mitch cocked his head and studied the victim's

wrists, looking for bruises or anything else out of the ordinary. A frown tugged at his mouth as he considered the wounds. The angled slash on her right wrist looked wrong somehow. Too deep...too brutal. He felt Alex move closer to him. She had regained her composure, he supposed. She'd looked a little shaky at first, but she'd proven tougher than he'd expected.

"Take a look at this," he said without glancing up.

She crouched next to him and he nodded toward the part that nagged at him. "That's a little reckless. Don't you think?" He gave Alex a moment to visually examine the mark before he continued. "This sort of suicide is usually well thought out. The details precise, ritualistic."

"That's generally the case," Alex agreed. Her face had regained some of its color, but she still looked a little washed out. She visually examined the victim closely, and then the room. "Where are her clothes?"

Mitch looked around, then called out to the detective in charge, "Wells!"

"Yo." Wells stuck his head in the door.

"Did you find the clothes she was wearing?"

"We found a pair of jeans, panties and a Cubs T-shirt in the hamper there." He motioned toward the wicker basket sitting between the toilet and the lavatory. "They've been bagged for forensics."

"Suicide note?" Alex asked as she braced her hands on her knees and pushed to her feet.

Wells reached into his inside jacket pocket and produced a bagged note. "Pretty straightforward stuff."

Mitch stood and read the note over Alex's shoulder. Jasna had given up on finding her sister. She felt responsible for allowing something to happen to her younger sibling and decided she could not live with the guilt. She had no one or nothing left.

"Do you recognize her handwriting?" Mitch asked Alex.

She nodded. "It's hers. She couldn't come up with the required retainer, so she wrote Victoria a letter thanking her for agreeing to take her case anyway shortly before I started my investigation."

The Colby Agency was doing this one for free. Mitch hadn't considered that. He knew their reputation. He wouldn't even hazard a guess as to what kind of retainer fee they commanded. He supposed this sort of thing was a good tax write-off. Or maybe, he admitted reluctantly, Victoria Colby was just what she appeared to be, a woman of compassion and scruples.

Alex handed the note back to Wells. She squatted next to the tub again and took another look at the victim. "What's this?" She pointed to the girl's fingernails. "It doesn't look like flesh."

Mitch knelt next to her and looked closely. Something white was caked under the nails of the victim's left hand.

Alex twisted around, studying the edge of the tub, the floor, and then the lavatory. She gestured to what appeared to be a small blood smear on the edge of the porcelain basin. She pushed to her feet. Mitch contemplated the smear a little longer, then stood.

Several long seconds passed while Alex studied the basin and the items there, a bar of soap and a toothbrush. She was completely focused, and extremely careful not to touch anything.

"Look at the bar of soap," she said finally.

Mitch leaned closer to inspect the white bar. Gouge marks marred its surface. Four of them to be exact.

Fingernail gouges. "Wells, you might want to bag this bar of soap."

Wells pressed between them, surveying the object in question. "The knife was in the tub. If that's—" he nodded to the soap "—what's under her nails, she must have done it before she did the slicing and dicing."

Mitch winced at Wells's word choice.

Alex shook her head. "Then why the blood here?" She pointed to the tiny smear on the edge of the basin.

Wells squatted down and looked closer. "Could be blood. The lab'll tell us for sure." He frowned as he stood, pulled a glove from his pocket and tugged it on. Carefully, he picked up the soap and turned it over. A tinge of red mingled with the wet residue on its underside. Wells swore. "Guess we missed that."

"Check the floor between here and there," Alex told him, indicating the tub. "I'll bet you find traces of blood there, too. And in the basin's S-trap."

Wells shrugged. "I don't know why she would have gotten out of the tub to wash her hands after she'd done the job."

"Maybe she didn't," Alex offered. "Maybe someone did it for her."

"Let's get this bagged," Wells said then, quickly escaping Alex's scrutiny.

"Look," Mitch said quietly, drawing Alex's attention. "It takes someone on the edge to want to take their own life." He could see the renewed effect this scene was having on Alex and he didn't like it. She was twisting the situation around, making it what she wanted it to be—a murder. "Are you sure Jasna was stable enough to give you the real facts? Maybe her sister left of her own free will after all. Maybe she doesn't want to be found. Maybe she and Jasna had a falling out. Despite these little anomalies, you have to know how this looks.''

Alex looked straight at him, those amber eyes glittering with determination. ''I don't believe she took her own life.'' She shook her head. ''It doesn't make sense. Why would she beg for help, then commit suicide when that help was at hand?''

''Maybe something happened this week that changed everything. Something you don't remember. You can't be sure that she didn't lose all hope. The fact is that you don't know when you last spoke with her or what mental state she was in at the time.''

''You're right about that,'' Alex agreed, to his complete surprise. ''But, I can't shake the notion that I'm right about this.''

''I've never put much stock in women's intuition,'' Mitch said wryly.

She glared at him. ''I'm talking about instinct, Hayden.'' She glanced at the woman who'd been her client, then back at Mitch. ''You know what I'm talking about. You can feel it, too. That little voice that keeps telling you that something about all this doesn't fit. Just listen, you'll hear it.''

ALEX REMAINED QUIET on the ride back to Shady Grove. Mitch knew he'd pushed her buttons with the women's intuition remark. Hell, he'd done it intentionally. Though he couldn't fully explain why he'd purposely riled her. He'd never been a masochist, why start now?

Because her anger was his only protection against those other crazy feelings, he realized with sudden clarity. He clenched his jaw and forced the unbidden thought away. The tension was getting to him.

"How soon will the preliminary autopsy be available?"

The sound of her husky voice broke the silence, yanking Mitch from his musings. "I asked Wells to let us know as soon as he knows. Tomorrow maybe. I can't say for sure."

"I want you to be straight with me on this investigation, Hayden. Don't keep me in the dark."

Something in her voice, desperation, maybe, made him want to reach out to her. Mitch squashed that yearning. "You keep Ashton off my back and I'll keep you informed."

"I'm sending him back to Chicago," she said quietly.

Surprised for the second time today, Mitch turned to her as he slowed for a red light. "I don't think he's going to like that."

She didn't look at Mitch. "He's a distraction. I don't need him here."

So, Mitch was right. There was something going on between her and Ashton. Knowing he'd been right failed to give Mitch any pleasure. "We should stop by the hospital and let them change that bandage."

"I want to talk to Zach first."

This was one goodbye Mitch couldn't wait to witness.

"I DON'T THINK this is a good idea," Zach repeated for the third time. He glanced at Mitch Hayden through the glass wall dividing the sheriff's office from the reception area. The blinds were open and Hayden was sitting on the edge of his receptionist's desk doing little to conceal the fact that he was watching their tense exchange.

Alex exhaled an impatient breath. She wasn't sure who she was more disgusted with—Zach or Hayden. "Look," she said, drawing her old friend's attention back to her. "I know you're worried about me, but I can take care of myself."

Blue eyes, the ones she'd once gotten lost in so easily, stared back at her now. "How can you expect me to just leave you here and pretend that everything's fine? Whoever took that shot at you will likely try again. You still don't have your memory back. How can I be sure Hayden will keep you safe?" Zach stepped closer, trying to see more than she wanted him to. He read her too easily.

He shook his head at what he no doubt saw. "I don't trust him, Al. I don't understand why you do."

She took his hand in hers. He squeezed her fingers, the gesture totally platonic. "No backwoods sheriff is going to get the best of me. I can hold my own with him. The one thing I feel confident about is that he'll do whatever he has to in order to keep me safe. I'm all he's got between two dead deputies and their killer." Alex resisted the urge to look at Hayden then. She could feel him watching her. The bloom of warmth that accompanied his close observation only flustered her all the more.

And that was the last thing she needed right now.

Zach ran a hand through his short, dark hair. "Victoria isn't going to like this. Jasna's death didn't help. She sent me down here to help you clear up this mess. How am I supposed to go back and tell her that you're still under suspicion for murder? That you can't remember the last six days and that some good-old-boy sheriff has the hots for you?"

Alex felt the color rise in her cheeks. "Zach, get real. I'm a suspect and or witness. That's all."

Zach's response was uncharacteristically crude.

"Well, that was constructive," she retorted impatiently.

"I'm not feeling particularly constructive at the moment." He shoved his hands into his pockets and studied her for a long time. "You're sure about this?"

"Yes," she said without reservation. "I need Hayden cooperative. How am I going to accomplish that with the two of you going head-to-head at every turn? I'm up to this, Zach. Your presence will only hamper the investigation." She sighed, flaring her hands in exasperation. "Victoria only sent you because of me. You know she needs you in Chicago."

He stared at the floor for a time before he responded. "If I go back and anything happens to you—"

"Nothing is going to happen." Alex smiled. "I'm in protective custody. Hayden isn't going to let me out of his sight."

"That's the part that worries me," Zach said grimly.

"I swear, Ashton, you sound like a jealous husband," she teased.

He touched her cheek as tenderly as he would have a child's. "You know how much you mean to me, Al. You're like the sister I never had."

That was true. They had mistaken that close bond for a time, but both of them had quickly realized that they weren't meant to be anything more than friends. "I have to do this." She chewed her lip for a second while she gathered her thoughts. "I'm having little flashes of recall already. I think if I concentrate on retracing my steps it'll all come back to me." She shrugged. "This is a small town, finding witnesses to my activities shouldn't be that difficult.'' There was no way to know what had become of her casebook. It wasn't among the personal belongings of which Mitch had allowed her to retake possession.

"I don't want you going it alone," Zach insisted. "I don't like it."

Alex tugged on his silk tie. "I'll be okay. But I need Delaney to do me a favor."

"Name it."

"He should be back in the city by now. When he's had time to complete his report on the Henshaw case, ask him to look into Phillip Malloy's background for me. I want to go all the way back to before the man was even a gleam in his daddy's eye. I want to know everything." And Ethan Delaney was just the investigator to do it. No one at the agency was more persistent.

At Zach's questioning look, she explained, "I've probably already done this myself, but I can't remember and who knows where my casebook is. If I found anything, it's stuck somewhere in all that scrambled gray matter. And I doubt I'll get the chance to dig around in Malloy's background with Hayden dogging my every step."

"Good point. Don't worry, if Delaney isn't available, I'll take care of it myself."

"Thanks, Zach." Alex smiled, relieved that he'd acquiesced to her wishes. "I knew I could count on you to understand."

He still looked uncertain. "If you need anything…"

"I'll call." Alex hugged him as if she might never see him again. She envied the woman who eventually snagged him. Zach Ashton was the best.

HIS TEETH HURT from clenching them so tightly, Mitch realized, frustrated to the point of wanting to throw something. He forced himself to relax when Alex finally released her enthusiastic hold on Ashton. Mitch swore under his breath. He didn't care that the two of them had a thing going. His dislike for Ashton had absolutely nothing to do with Alex. Ashton was a big-city attorney who thought he could come down here and tell Mitch how to run his investigation. That was the source of the animosity. Nothing more.

The last couple of days had taken their toll on Mitch. That's all. He wasn't himself.

Mitch wanted Ashton on the road so he could get on with the investigation without unwanted interference. He had no hidden motivation or agenda. Alex was a suspect.

Ashton stepped back from the embrace he'd shared with Alex and glanced at his watch. When he looked up, his gaze shifted in Mitch's direction for a nanosecond. Their gazes locked for that infinitesimal space in time, and something distinctly adversarial passed between them. Without missing a beat, Ashton's right hand went up and wrapped around Alex's neck. He pulled her to him and kissed her firmly on the mouth.

A kind of quake rocked through Mitch. Fury followed in its wake. All that kept him anchored in place was his white-knuckle grasp on the edge of the desk on which he was sitting. The meshing of lips only lasted a moment. But that was a second too long. Ashton's gaze landed squarely on Mitch's then, a clear warning.

Mitch stood. An instinctive meeting of the challenge that had been silently issued. The door opened then and the two made their way out to where he waited.

"There's a one-thirty commercial flight back to Chicago, so I don't see any point in having Victoria send the jet back down for me," Ashton said, his expression entirely too smug for Mitch's liking. "I guess I'll be on it since Alex doesn't need me here."

"Leaving already?" Mitch quipped. "That's a shame."

Zach stepped in closer to him and spoke for Mitch's ears only. "You let anything happen to her, Hayden, and I'll be back. *For you*," he added with a lethal look that left nothing to the imagination as to what he meant.

Mitch met that deadly gaze without blinking. "Don't worry, Ashton, I'll take good care of her. She's my only link to two murders. I'm not about to let anything happen to her." Not to mention Nashville P.D. would likely need to question her further in the Bukovak suicide.

"I want her back in Chicago as soon as this is over."

"You have my word on it," Mitch told him flatly. "I'll clear her of any charges and put her on a plane headed north, or I'll lock her up and throw away the key. Either way, I'll have an answer." He paused for emphasis. "Soon."

Mitch ignored the distress signals emanating from Alex. He couldn't say whether she was anxious over he and Ashton's war of wills or Mitch's pronouncement that he intended to solve this case at any cost. Whatever concerned her, he was through being ruled by emotions he didn't understand. He had a double homicide to solve. Two men he respected and called friends were dead. And one way or another this little city gal was going to lead him to their killer.

MITCH SCANNED the interview reports and preliminary forensic findings from the two shootings scattered across his kitchen table. It was after midnight and he was exhausted. He rubbed at his bleary eyes. He had nothing. Ballistics had confirmed that the rifle Roy had found in Alex's hotel room was indeed the one used to kill Saylor. But there were no prints. Not one. The serial number had been filed off the rifle.

The shooter was a professional. But why? It didn't make sense. Nothing about Miller or his lifestyle could possibly have garnered the interest of anyone capable of hiring an assassin. The same could be said for Saylor, though Mitch hadn't known him his entire life as he had Miller.

Alex had to be the key. Maybe the shootings had nothing to do with the Bukovak case Alex came to Shady Grove to investigate. Mitch stilled, allowing the thought to solidify. Maybe someone from a previous Colby Agency case was out for revenge. That would explain the apparent setup attempt. The rifle sure as hell hadn't been in her room the first time they looked.

Then again, Alex could be in on it.

But why? There was no motivation.

Disgusted, Mitch pushed up from the table. He stalked over to the sink and leaned against the counter to stare out into the dark night. None of this made any sense. It had to be someone after Alex. Something totally unconnected to this county and the men who had died for no real reason. The instinct that had never failed him before nagged at him now. That scenario didn't quite fit either. Why would anyone seeking revenge against Alex choose here and now to make his move? Taking out a P.I. was one thing, but murdering two deputies was another. A capital offense to be exact.

And then there was the Bukovak girl's suicide. It just didn't make sense.

Mitch had tried to convince himself that at least Miller's death was no mystery. After all, Alex's prints were on the murder weapon and the powder residue on her skin indicated that she had definitely been holding the weapon when it was fired. But that scenario wasn't cut and dried either. The residue pattern was not conclusive. In fact, it was barely there. The forensics report stated unconditionally that the residue on her skin was not consistent with those expected under typical circumstances with the particular weapon used. Mitch had studied that report forward and backward. The bottom line, in his opinion, was that someone might have been holding her hand when the weapon fired.

There had to be a third party involved in Miller's death. The same person who fired the rifle and killed Saylor. And, whoever it was, he or she was no friend of Alex Preston's. Now all Mitch had to figure out was whether the case was related to the Bukovak girl, which he considered unlikely, or the Colby Agency.

That was one mystery he wouldn't be able to solve tonight. He was burned out. Mitch crossed the room and switched off the light. Though he'd never felt compelled to lock his doors in the past, he did so tonight. It irked him that anything could intrude on the small-town life he cherished so. For the most part, people didn't have to worry about locking their doors around here. But things were different now. Alex Preston had brought big-city problems with her when she showed up in his county.

He paused at the door of his spare room and looked in on her. She was sleeping soundly. Long dark hair spilled across her pillow. The bulky bandage on her forehead had been replaced by a much smaller one. He'd taken her by the hospital to have it checked after they'd dropped Ashton off at the airport. There was the one good thing about this whole damned day, Mitch mused. Ashton was out of his way.

The memory of Ashton kissing Alex loomed large in Mitch's mind, rekindling a fury he shouldn't feel. This was entirely too screwed up. There was absolutely no reason for him to feel possessive of Alex on a personal level. A few hours of chitchat over dinner shouldn't have made this kind of impact.

Sure she was attractive—more than attractive—but he'd had his share of attractive women. She was smart, but so were the other women he dated. But there was something about this one. He closed his eyes and silently cursed himself. Something that touched a place way down deep inside him, made him want to reach out to her.

And, like the two murders currently haunting him, he couldn't explain it.

It simply was.

Shaking his head, Mitch turned away from the woman who made him so restless. He was already taking a huge risk bringing her here. If someone really was trying to kill her, they would come here, to his home, after her. Mitch hadn't missed the odd looks he'd gotten when it became clear to his staff that he was bringing Alex home with him. He didn't need suspicions being cast among his men. But he also wasn't about to leave Alex in a cell.

There was another point he had no intention of analyzing too deeply tonight.

He would just have to figure all that out tomorrow. And, if he was lucky, maybe Alex would remember something.

Like who killed Deputy Miller.

Chapter Four

At 3:00 a.m. Mitch jerked awake. He glanced at the digital clock on the bedside table, all the while listening intently for whatever it was that had awakened him. Silence echoed through the house like the hollow sound that emanates from a deep well.

He sat up and threw the covers back. He was a light sleeper and he couldn't ignore what his senses were telling him. Something was wrong. Though he couldn't say what he'd heard, if anything, some anomaly in the night had yanked him from dreamland. Which was just as well, he decided dropping his feet to the floor. He'd been dreaming about sex. His body was as hard as a rock and throbbing for satisfaction, which didn't help.

Nor did the fact that the subject of his sensual fantasies was his current houseguest.

He tugged on his jeans but didn't bother to fasten them since that would only add to his discomfort. Crossing the room he forked his fingers through his hair and pushed it back from his face. He stalled at the door when another low, indistinguishable sound reached him.

Alex cried out again, snapping him back into action.

A few steps later and he was in her room. She barreled straight into him just inside the door.

"Whoa!" Mitch steadied her trembling body. "It's okay," he assured her, assuming she'd had herself a bad dream.

"I have to go outside," she urged, trying to pull away from him. "I need air."

He couldn't see her eyes in the dark, but he could hear the sheer terror in her voice. Whatever she'd been dreaming about, it had scared the hell out of her and panic had taken over.

"Take a deep breath and calm down. We'll go out onto the porch." As she inhaled deeply, he ushered her into the hall and toward the front door. She held that breath for a few seconds before releasing it slowly. "That's good," he encouraged. "Now take another and stay right here until I tell you otherwise."

He unlocked the door and stepped onto the porch. He surveyed the moonlit yard and the trees beyond. Under the cover of the porch it was as dark as pitch.

"All right, you can come out."

She bolted through the door. Mitch kept a bit of distance between them. She didn't appear to want to make a run for it, she just stood on the edge of the porch in the dark gulping in the fresh night air.

Finally, she sank onto the top step. He sat down next to her. The theory that someone was trying to kill her flitted through his mind again, but he dismissed it. It was still only a theory. Besides, no one but his deputies knew where Alex was. Even if someone were out there, he'd have to be using night vision to see them. And if he was right about his assumptions, whoever had been after Alex was long gone now that he knew he'd killed an officer of the law. Mitch doubted that any revenge the shooter might be seeking against the Colby Agency ran deep enough to risk facing a capital murder charge.

Mitch studied Alex's profile in the moonlight that spilled over the steps. Her dark hair was mussed, her hands still trembling when she pushed it behind her ears. Her eyes were large and long-lashed and the line of her nose was in perfect proportion to her other facial features. But the lips were the part that drew his attention like a beacon in the night. Full, with a delicious natural color that made him think of shiny red apples. The kind of lips movie stars paid the big bucks for. The fact that she was wearing a T-shirt for a nightgown only added to the appeal of the image and did nothing to lessen the heaviness in his groin. He kept his gaze carefully averted from those long toned legs.

"Feel better now?"

"Yeah, thanks," she murmured, her voice as shaky as her hands.

For a long while she sat there, staring up at the brilliant sky. The stars were still twinkling like uncut diamonds scattered across a black velvet canvas. Mitch was relatively sure they didn't have skies like this in the city. Only in the wide-open spaces of the country could you see a sight like this. He wondered if she was as much in awe of it as he was of her.

"He was wearing a black ski mask," she said, shattering the silence that had lengthened between them.

Mitch shifted his focus back to that lovely profile. Her brow was creased in concentration, those full lips drawn down into a frown. She drew in a ragged breath, struggling to remember that night filled with unspeakable terror. Terror he'd only theorized about at this point. He wanted desperately to reach out to her, but he resisted. He had to keep this relationship clear of intimate entrapments. Chemistry. That's all it was anyway. A man and a woman getting a little too close.

"Was there anything about him you recognized?" he prodded, focusing on business. "Think about how he smelled, the sound of his voice if he spoke. Did any of it strike a chord of recognition?"

She flinched. "He hit me." She jerked again as if vividly recalling the blow. "Over and over. He wouldn't stop. I tried to fight back, but then..." Alex swiped at her eyes. "I can't remember."

She didn't speak for a time, then eventually began again. "I could hear someone yelling in the background but it wasn't the guy who was hitting me. It was someone else...another man."

Mitch kept his hands tightly clasped between his spread thighs to keep from reaching out to her. "Close your eyes and think about the smells, the sounds, other than the voice."

She obeyed, concentrating hard with the effort. "Exhaust fumes," she said eventually. "There was a car running in the background."

"Anything else?"

She shook her head. "It's pretty fuzzy. Just snippets of movement and emotion. Nothing I can nail down." She shivered, from her memories or the cold, he couldn't be sure. "Maybe I'm afraid to remember."

Alex stood before he could respond to that statement, turning her attention back to the night sky, a much safer, more comforting subject. Mitch pushed up beside her. When she shivered again he couldn't help himself, he touched her. Just the slightest caress of her bare arm. Electricity sizzled along his fingertips.

"You should go back inside and try to get some more sleep."

She turned to him, her eyes searching his, trying to evaluate what it was he was offering with that touch. "I appreciate you allowing me to stay here rather than in a cell or at the hospital."

Mitch tamped down the impulse to trace that fading bruise on her left cheek. "As long as you don't give me any trouble you're welcome to stay. When I told Ashton I would take care of you, I meant it."

"You don't believe I killed Miller, do you?"

The question caught him off guard. "I haven't decided what I think just yet," he lied. "You're still a suspect."

She laughed softly. "You know I didn't do it. You're only keeping me around to see if you can draw out the real killer. I know what you're up to, Sheriff. And I don't mind. I want him just as badly as you do because somehow he's connected to Marija's disappearance. And maybe even to Jasna's alleged suicide."

"That's a pretty big leap considering the lack of connection," he countered. And she was right, he did hope that keeping her around would draw out the killer...if he hadn't disappeared already. If there was any chance of catching the guy, Mitch wanted to take full advantage of it. He just hadn't admitted on a conscious level that Alex was his bait. Bait he intended to keep safe at all costs. "How do you know that the guy didn't follow you from Chicago? This could be some sort of vendetta resulting from an old Colby Agency case."

She considered that possibility for a moment. "Maybe, but I doubt it. It just doesn't feel right. This is about the case I came here to work on. It has to be."

"Maybe," he echoed her response. "But then again, maybe not."

"Good night, Sheriff," she said, clearly uninterested in pursuing the disagreement.

Before Mitch could think of a good enough reason to stop her she was across the porch and at the door. She paused before going inside and looked back at him.

"I'd like to go to where it happened," she said bluntly. "Can we do that today?"

The doctor had said not to try and force anything, to let the memories come on their own. "I'm not sure that's the right thing to do." Another part of him wanted to do just that. To speed up the process and get this investigation over with so he could get on with his life and get Alex Preston out of it.

"I need to see it. I need to be there." She returned his steady gaze with a determined one of her own. "I also want to talk to the TBI agent in charge of the serial killings you told me about. And, if possible, I want to see the man accused of the crimes."

A startled laugh choked out of Mitch. "You expect me to get you an appointment with Waylon Gill? Even if that were possible, I don't see what it would accomplish." Mitch strode slowly toward her. "What on earth would you say to him?" He hadn't meant that last remark to come out in such a patronizing tone, but it had and it was too late to take it back.

"Just get me the appointment," she insisted, her tone openly challenging. "You'll be surprised at what I can accomplish."

Before Mitch could say anything else she whirled around and stomped inside. He swore at his own stupidity. How could he walk away from a challenge like that? If he didn't at least try to get her the appointment then he couldn't disprove her theories or her professed abilities.

He had no choice.

Locking the door behind him, he headed back to his own bed. Give her enough rope and she would hang herself, he decided. Once she'd gotten these ridiculously far-fetched scenarios out of her system, then maybe the memories would come flooding back. Mitch had done a little reading up on retrograde amnesia. Most of the time a victim could put off the inevitable by convincing herself that there was another answer for her problems.

Alex would prove no exception.

ALEX SURVEYED the forest that closed in on either side of the road. The changing colors of the leaves added splashes of contrasting hues here and there breaking the monopoly of green. The canopy of thick boughs blocked most of the midmorning sunlight, casting the unpaved road in shadows. The occasional glint of sun sliced through nature's covering like shafts of polished steel.

Just like yesterday in Jasna's room, her chest felt too heavy, too tight. Alex had the sudden overwhelming urge to run. She focused on the driver and did all in her power to slow her heart's fierce pounding. Hayden had promised to keep her safe. She had no reason to doubt his word. Something about him made her feel safe…made her trust him instinctively. Something more than the badge he wore. A flash of his handsome face lined in anger flitted through her thoughts, but she dismissed the senseless bit as insignificant. She was the only witness he had at the moment, he wasn't about to let anything happen to her. At least not until he had some answers.

The Jeep slowed and he turned left onto a narrow

passage that fell well short of her definition of a road. That sense of impending doom enveloped her all over again. Hayden parked the vehicle maybe ten feet from a small clearing. The whole area had been cordoned off with the customary yellow tape.

"They impounded your rental car and Miller's vehicle for the forensics guys to scour."

She'd known they would do that. She hadn't expected the vehicles to still be here. Though it might have helped her visualize if they had been in place.

Alex slid out of the Jeep. She scanned the so-called road behind her, then the vehicle in which she'd arrived. The image of a gray sedan abruptly seared into her mind. She was climbing out of the car on the driver's side. She was looking around, trying her best not to appear as scared as she felt. The remembered uneasiness slid through her even now.

"Did you hear what I said?"

The sound of Hayden's voice jerked her from the strange dreamlike state. "What?" She blinked repeatedly in an effort to bring him into focus.

"Your car was parked here." He gestured to his Jeep. "Miller's was parked a few feet farther up."

Feeling lost and yet somehow as if she knew her way, Alex moved toward the clearing. Unintelligible voices whispered inside her head. Snippets of indistinguishable images sifted through as well. She stood in the middle of the clearing and turned around slowly. Her eyes closed and the voices grew louder, the images grew more vivid.

You're going to kill her. Dammit. You didn't say anything about killing her.

The breath flew out of her lungs at the memory of a booted foot slamming into her abdomen. The memory was so vivid Alex gasped. She clutched her stomach and doubled over. She could hear Hayden calling out to her but she couldn't answer. The back of a hand collided with her cheek. She jerked back uncertain whether it was real or imagined. *That's enough!* the male voice she recalled so well shouted. She staggered, pain roaring through her body, dizziness threatening her ability to stay vertical. The ground rushed up to meet her. Strong fingers closed around her throat, jerking her up, then slamming her against a tree. Pain exploded in the back of her head and everything went black.

Mitch fell to his knees next to Alex. Her body jerked and quivered. He pulled her into his arms and held her close. "Alex! Can you hear me?" Her entire body suddenly tensed, then went bonelessly limp against him.

What the hell was happening? He scooped her up and pushed to his feet. He had to get her to the hospital. His heart pounding so loud he could hardly hear himself think, Mitch settled her into the passenger seat and fastened the seat belt around her. He checked to make sure her breathing was steady. She was out cold and her pulse was rapid. Her skin felt clammy.

Mitch rounded the hood and jumped behind the wheel. He broke every speed limit he'd sworn to uphold getting to the hospital. By the time he roared up to the emergency entrance, Alex was coming around.

He bounded out of the vehicle and hurried to her side. She crumpled against his chest when he pulled her into his arms once more. His gut tied in knots at the helpless feeling that swamped him. He should never have taken her to that clearing. The doctor had warned against forcing the memories. Mitch knew better. It didn't matter that it was her idea. The bottom line was he shouldn't have allowed it.

Already at the hospital seeing another patient and to Mitch's utter relief, the neurologist was on his way to the E.R. within minutes. The doctor ordered a second CT scan just to make sure nothing new was going on. Then he did a routine reflex screening.

"Everything appears to be in order, Ms. Preston," Dr. Reynor announced. "It's not unusual for an amnesia patient to experience a mild seizure during an emotionally traumatic period like this."

Mild? The episode had scared the hell out of Mitch. He breathed his first sigh of relief since seeing her go down in that clearing. He'd paced like a caged animal in this tiny exam room while he waited for the doctor to finish.

"You're sure she's okay?" he demanded, knowing full well the doctor had already given him the answer.

Dr. Reynor patted Mitch on the shoulder. "Really, Sheriff, she's fine. The fact that some of her memory is coming back already is a good sign. I know you're in a hurry to get this case solved, but recapturing the lost time can't be rushed. As I told you before, whatever comes will come in its own time."

"The memories aren't specific," Alex told him, breaking into the conversation for the first time. "They're more like feelings."

The doctor nodded. "The detail will come." His brow furrowed in concern. "With events this traumatic it would be in your best interest not to rush it, Ms. Preston. I can't caution you strongly enough to take it slow and easy. And you shouldn't be alone. Like today, you might need assistance during a particularly vivid recall."

"Don't worry," Mitch cut in. "She won't be alone."

ALEX LEANED BACK into the seat of Mitch's Jeep and tried to relax. Her visit to the scene of the crime hadn't gone anything like she'd expected. Sensory overload had sent her into a seizure. That wasn't something she wanted to repeat anytime soon. The episode had left her weak and disoriented. Almost two hours later she was still feeling a little out of it. Dr. Reynor had insisted on keeping her at the hospital for observation for an hour.

She glanced at her watch and realized the time. The appointment Hayden had made with the TBI agent was in less than one hour. "How far is it to the prison?"

"Forget it," Hayden snapped. "There's no way I'm subjecting you to any other stressors today."

Fury washed over her. "It isn't your choice."

Hayden shot her a look, those blue eyes icy with challenge. "You wanna bet? I made the appointment. I can cancel it."

Alex searched for calm. She had to appeal to his sense of reason. "Just because Jasna is dead doesn't mean I don't intend to follow through with my investigation. The only way I can disprove your uncle's involvement is to show that her sister's disappearance was related to Gill's killing spree."

That should do it, Alex thought, giving herself a mental pat on the back.

Fury instantly melted the ice in those cool blue eyes, turning them the color of molten steel. "We've had this conversation already. You will not drag my uncle's name through the mud. I won't allow it. The girl was fine when Phillip and Nadine took her to the airport."

A muscle ticked rhythmically in his tense jaw, lending a dangerous quality to his annoyingly attractive features. Just what she needed, a keeper who was too good-looking and entirely too sexy for his own good—or hers.

"Then let me prove that theory is a bust. You take me to this appointment and I guarantee I'll walk away knowing whether or not Gill is involved in Marija's disappearance."

He cast her a doubting looking. "You can't make a guarantee like that."

Alex smiled. "Just sit back and watch, Sheriff."

Two hours later Mitch and Agent Talkington, the TBI agent in charge of Gill's investigation, watched in amazement as Alex conversed with Waylon Gill on the other side of the two-way mirror.

"She's good," Talkington remarked.

"Yeah." She was that. *I guarantee I'll walk away knowing whether or not Gill is involved*...reverberated in Mitch's mind.

Though Gill was fully shackled, Mitch still felt uneasy about him being alone in an interview room with Alex. But she had insisted that she needed one-on-one with the monster. The guy gave Mitch the creeps.

Gill was reed thin and gangly. His face was average, not particularly handsome or ugly. Brown hair, brown eyes and no distinguishing marks. He smiled a lot, had good teeth and a quiet voice. There was nothing noticeably frightening or unusual about the thirty-five-year-old man. Like most serial killers, he was above average in intelligence and could talk his way into a convent even if he was wearing a tail and horns and waving a pitchfork. But the man was a sociopath Mitch could have gone the rest of his life without meeting.

Gill had brutally raped and murdered at least six young female college students. His M.O. was a sick ritual that prolonged the agony of his victims. His trial was still months away, but he had already confessed to the six counts of premeditated murder. He just wasn't owning up to any others. The profiler from Quantico who'd worked with the TBI on the case felt certain there were more victims that might never be found. Since Gill had only lived in the area for a couple of years, it was expected that more bodies would turn up in the towns where he'd lived previously. Mitch wasn't sure he bought that scenario.

And Gill wasn't talking. Well, except in riddles. Talkington had indicated that the man loved crossword puzzles and riddles. Most of the clues he dropped were coded in his own warped personal encryption. He dared the investigators working his case to try and solve the mystery of him. But Mitch had the guy's number already—he was a frigging psycho, end of story.

"I've heard about the Colby Agency," Talkington said after a few minutes. "Top-notch group. If she's any indication of the caliber of investigators they employ, I can see why."

"Is that why you agreed to allow her to interview him?"

Talkington nodded. "Partly." He shrugged. "And partly because I wanted to see how Gill would react to a new face."

Mitch didn't say anything. He didn't like Talkington's motivation. But Mitch was already far too taken with this particular P.I., he didn't need to demonstrate it further by making some protective remark. It was bad enough that he couldn't take his eyes off her. She was smart, gutsy and gorgeous. She'd gained his respect in record time, which wasn't an easy feat. This little party only added to his growing awe. The last thing he needed was to start trusting her. It was definitely too soon for that. Especially considering the way she had fooled him before.

"Hell," Talkington went on, "Gill's said more to her in the past twenty minutes than he did to us after hours of interrogation. 'Course that profiler the Feds sent me didn't look anything like this pretty young thing." He chuckled wryly. "Shoot, Gill's probably enjoying this little tête-à-tête."

"You find that thought humorous, Talkington?"

The man squirmed beneath Mitch's drop-dead glare. "Well, you have to admit, he does look happy."

The hell of it was, Talkington was right. Mitch glared at the man seated across the table from Alex. Gill was smiling widely, probably getting off right there in the room uncaring of who was watching. Alex was charming him the same way she'd charmed Mitch that first night they'd met. Ire twisted inside him. He wanted this over. But Alex appeared in no hurry.

"YOU'RE AWFULLY PRETTY for a cop," Gill said in a slightly shy tone that had likely won him the trust of too many unwary young girls.

"Thank you." Alex studied him for a moment. She was always amazed at just how normal a man who murdered for pleasure and without conscience could appear. "I have a friend I think you'll find even more attractive." Alex opened the folder she'd brought with her. She'd laid it on the desk when she entered the room then rested her clasped hands on top of it so that he would know she had something to show him before she mentioned it.

"Let me see," he urged, impatient for more visual stimuli.

He'd shown avid interest from the moment Alex walked through the door. It sickened her to think that he was probably sitting there with an erection right now. Forcing the thought away and watching Gill closely, she offered him the glossy headshot of Marija Bukovak. The photograph was her graduation picture.

"Isn't she pretty?"

"Mmm." He studied the photograph with open interest, but absolutely no outward response. "She sure is. What's her name?" Instinctively he flipped the picture over and looked at the back.

"Her name is Marija Bukovak. She just graduated from a high school not too far from here."

"Very, very pretty," he said as he passed the picture back to her. "But not my type."

Careful not to show any reaction, Alex tucked the photograph back into the folder. "Why is that, Waylon? She's a lot prettier than I am."

That dark, bottomless gaze connected with hers in a way that made her want to run, but she held her ground. In the few seconds that ticked by before he spoke, Alex saw the evil, saw the insatiable appetite for the unspeakable in that wide, frank gaze.

"Can I tell you a secret?" he murmured, leaning across the table, closer to her.

Her heart pounding like a drum, Alex leaned nearer, her gaze never deviating from his, their foreheads almost touching. "You can tell me anything, Waylon. And it'll be our secret."

He hunched his shoulders to draw even closer to her. Close enough that she could smell the toothpaste on his breath. She could see the sprinkling of freckles across his nose that, added to his easy smile, made him look like the all-American guy. There was absolutely nothing about Waylon Gill that would give a girl advance notice to run for her life unless he chose to allow her to see it in his eyes. He was almost charming…*almost.*

"I never, ever touch a woman," he whispered, "no matter how beautiful, unless she's really smart. If she's not in college, you can forget it. If she's not as smart as me, then there's no challenge. Anybody can pick up a naive high school girl and fool her." His perpetual smile widened into a knowing grin. "But I need the challenge. What's the point otherwise?"

He angled his head still closer to her, drawing in her breath. Blatantly savoring the smell of her. "Now you, you're a different story." He made a sound of satisfaction in his throat. "I could do things to you that would shock even the friends you've got watching behind that mirror."

Alex started to pull away. But she couldn't move fast enough to dodge his intention. His teeth clamped down on her already bruised cheek. She jerked out of his reach, tumbling backward in her chair.

Gill's laughter echoed around her, filling the now too-small room.

He shoved the table out of his way. She scrambled to put more distance between them.

"Are you scared, Alex?" he demanded, his tone no longer silky with charm, but harsh and frightening. He grabbed his crotch with his shackled hands. "I've got something for you, pretty lady."

Waylon Gill hurled himself at her.

Chapter Five

"I'm telling you he didn't do it," Alex insisted, her gaze tracking Mitch as he paced behind his desk.

Mitch stalled midstride and glared at her. He flattened his palms on his desk and leaned forward. She drew back in her chair as if she were afraid of what he intended. Mitch swore under his breath. The episode with Gill had shaken her more than even she realized. The ice pack had done little to alleviate the redness the son of a bitch had left on her cheek when he attacked her. At least he hadn't broken the skin, just left his mark. Fury twisted inside Mitch. He wanted to save the taxpayers some money and kill Waylon Gill with his bare hands.

"The guy is a frigging psycho. How can you be sure if anything he says is even remotely related to the truth?"

She lifted her chin a notch, regaining a bit of her self-assurance. "I just know." She closed her eyes for a second and sighed. "All of his victims were college students. He wouldn't change his routine."

"You can't be sure of that," Mitch argued, impatience roaring through him.

She focused that intent amber gaze on his. "He told

me the truth. If there are any other victims, they'll not only be college age, but enrolled.'' She touched her cheek, unconsciously tracing the imprint of the bastard's teeth. ''He watches them for days, weeks maybe. The victims he picks have to meet his standards. Beautiful, intelligent—''

''And available,'' Mitch interrupted. ''I know all that crap. It's in the profiler's report.''

She shook her head. ''Not necessarily available. If they were seeing someone else that would only add to the challenge of getting close to them.''

Mitch straightened and laughed, a rude, grating sound even to his own ears. ''Well, his little killing soiree in Davidson County proved too challenging, because he screwed up and got caught.''

''He didn't screw up. He wanted to be caught. It isn't always the case, but sometimes these guys want to be punished.''

''Oh, yeah.'' Mitch rolled his eyes. God, he hated all that psychobabble. ''How could I forget? It was a cry for help. Attacking you must have been a temporary relapse.''

''He couldn't resist the challenge I represented, that's all.''

Renewed fury ignited, sending Mitch's common sense scurrying for parts unknown. ''You really believe all that crap, don't you?'' He skirted his desk and settled on the edge of it directly in front of her. He folded his arms over his chest to keep from doing something totally stupid like grabbing her and shaking her. ''He could have hurt you a lot worse than he did and all you can say is that he couldn't resist?''

Mitch was angrier with himself than he was with her.

He should never have allowed her to go into that interview alone with the creep.

When she didn't respond right away, he added, "He's killed six women. How can you look at him and see anything other than pure evil that can't be trusted?"

"You're wrong," she said solemnly. "Waylon Gill is thirty-five-years old. He's killed a great deal more than six. They need to look more closely into his past. Start with his own early college days. I imagine he's told them, just not in a way they understand yet. He's playing a game. He wants to make them work for his full story."

Mitch could only stare at her. How could she possibly know this? Then he remembered what Talkington said. *Gill's said more to her in the past twenty minutes…*

"Why do you think so?"

Alex blinked, uncertain how to answer his question. How could she ever explain that she felt things a little more deeply than most? A macho guy like Hayden would never buy into that dog and pony show. She definitely didn't want to go into it now. Though she would never admit it, Gill had shaken her to the core. Her current physical and mental state obviously didn't lend itself to wrestling with a violent criminal. A loud rap against the door saved Alex from having to attempt an explanation.

"Sheriff, that conference call you've been expecting is on line two."

Alex was glad for the reprieve, though the call would prove a waste of time. First thing that morning Mitch had called Victoria's office and asked for a teleconference this afternoon to discuss any past cases that might be involved in Alex's current situation. Despite the fact that she didn't know precisely what had taken place three nights ago, she did know that it was related to the Bukovak case. No matter what Mitch thought, Alex could feel it. And she could only hope that he would not mention the episode with Gill to Victoria. The last thing she needed was Zach back down here holding her hand and going head-to-head with the sheriff. He'd put on enough of a territorial show with that kiss he'd laid on her yesterday. She'd been so startled she hadn't been able to react. The fact that he'd done it just to tick off Hayden had made her want to slap her good friend. Or maybe she needed to slap herself for not taking heed to Zach's warning.

"Thanks, Peg." Mitch reached across his desk and pulled the phone toward him. He punched the speaker button. "Hayden."

"Victoria Colby here, Sheriff. I have Zach Ashton and Ethan Delaney on my end. Is Alex there?"

Alex smiled, glad to hear a friendly voice. "I'm here, Victoria."

"Hey, Al." It was Ethan. "When you have a hard drive crash, you really have one. How's the memory bank?"

Trying her level best to block the macho vibes emanating from the guy standing over her, she focused on answering the question. "I'm still locked out, but I'm making progress."

The words were no more out of her mouth than she realized her mistake. Mitch eyed her suspiciously, as if she'd been holding out on him. She'd already explained that she hadn't remembered anything specific, but maybe he didn't believe her.

"I haven't remembered anything significant yet," she clarified quickly.

"Don't rush things, Al," Zach urged. "Take it slow."

"What did you come up with?" Mitch demanded impatiently and smoothly cutting off any response Alex might have made to Zach.

"I'll let Ethan fill you in," Victoria told him. "He's spent the entire day reviewing the cases Alex has worked over the past two years."

"The only two cases that involved anywhere near the level of emotion to motivate this kind of action," Ethan began, "were a couple of child custody disputes last year, but I've checked on the players and everything's cool."

"What about before that?" Mitch wanted to know. "She's worked at your agency for four years."

Alex stiffened. "I didn't start working in the field until two years ago," she said in hopes of cutting off what Ethan was likely going to say next. She didn't want Mitch Hayden to know her background. He would only ask questions. Questions she didn't care to answer.

"That's right," Ethan said, to her supreme annoyance. "Al worked in research the first year, and then in case profiling after that. She's the best. Quantico's tried to woo her back several times."

"Thanks, Ethan," she interjected. "Anything else?"

Quantico? Stunned, Mitch could only stare at the lady seated in front of him. Why hadn't she told him about that? Better yet, why was he surprised? She'd been keeping secrets right from the beginning. No wonder she knew her way around a crime scene so well. Not to mention how to conduct an interrogation.

"After your interview with Gill, do you still believe

he wasn't involved in Marija's disappearance?'' Victoria wanted to know.

Alex didn't hesitate. "Absolutely."

Had she learned something at Quantico that the other profiler hadn't? Mitch doubted it. "We're not ruling out that option," he added, which garnered him a questioning look from Alex. "The agent in charge of the Gill investigation is still leaning in that direction."

"That's because it's the easy way out," Ashton cut in. "If Alex says Gill didn't do it, then he didn't do it. You can take her word to the bank."

Mitch tamped down his temper. He would not let Ashton get to him today. "I'll bear that in mind."

"Alex, keep me posted," Victoria said. "I want to hear a status report from you every twenty-four hours, especially in light of Jasna's death."

"Thank you, Mrs. Colby, we'll do that," Mitch replied, steam building entirely too fast inside him. "Have a nice day." He stabbed the off button, then leveled a gaze he hoped relayed the depth of his irritation on Alex. "We have to talk."

Mitch Hayden didn't like surprises. That much was clear. Alex mentally counted to ten before she responded. She would not tell him that he was the rudest man she'd ever met. She didn't even get to say goodbye to her friends. She wouldn't say how much she despised being treated as if he, and only he, controlled her universe.

"What would you like to talk about?" she asked, feigning innocence.

He stood, a deliberate act of intimidation Alex intended to ignore. To even the playing field, she rose from her chair as well, putting herself toe-to-toe with him, and met his furious gaze.

"It seems you left out a few pertinent points about your background. Like the fact that you're a Farm graduate."

To slow her temper's ascent, Alex took a moment before responding. During that time, she studied the man who currently dominated her existence. The faded jeans, Titans T-shirt, and unbuttoned blue cotton chambray shirt he wore, not to mention the work boots, all served to give Mitch Hayden a very laid-back appearance. But he wasn't fooling Alex. She knew the kind of man he was. He was focused, ambitious and fiercely loyal to the job. Not bad qualities, just annoying at times.

This was one of those times.

As Alex retraced her visual path up his tall frame, there were a few things she tried her level best not to notice. Like the way his jeans fit his muscular body, or the way the width of his shoulders tested the seams of his shirt. Frames of memory flashed in her mind's eye. His bare chest, the feel of his skin, the clean masculine scent of him.

Her gaze collided with his then and she suddenly felt at a loss for what she wanted to say. She moistened her lips and dredged up a pathetic excuse for a response. "I didn't think it would make a difference."

That cool, analyzing gaze studied her too closely. She resisted the urge to squirm.

"I didn't know they trained civilians for anything other than future agents."

"I was with the Bureau for almost three years before I left to work with the Colby Agency." She had to find a way to change the subject before it went any further. "What about you?" she forged ahead. "What did you do before becoming the sheriff here?"

"We're not talking about me."

Alex chewed her lower lip, digging deep for all that she knew about the sheriff. "You're a third generation sheriff of Raleigh County. Your older brother tried the hat on for part of one term, but didn't find the job to his liking. As his chief deputy you were appointed to the position after that. You're up for election next year. But you're not worried because the Haydens have run this county for more than fifty years. You've never been married and your social life stinks." Startled by that last part, Alex held her breath in anticipation of his retaliation.

He looked as startled as she felt. "I'm flattered you find my life so fascinating."

Surprised that she'd defused his anger instead of fueling it, she went on, "I always like to know who I'm up against."

He lifted one tawny eyebrow a tad higher than the other. "Is that what we are? Against each other?"

"In a manner of speaking." Now he was digging. "You think I had something to do with the deaths of your two deputies, and I know I didn't."

"I see," he snapped. "You must have forgotten to tell me that you'd regained your memory of the events that night."

Well, Alex mused, it certainly didn't take much to inch his temper back up to the boiling point. "No, it's just instinct, I suppose."

He nodded, doubt written all over his face. "Like the instinct you have about Gill and Jasna?"

It was her anger that did the climbing this time. "Exactly."

"Look." He leaned closer, deliberately filling her personal space with his male arrogance. "Just because the folks in Chicago believe in those instincts of yours, doesn't mean I do. Down here, Ms. Preston, we operate on hard evidence, not speculation."

Alex smiled, a gesture totally lacking humor. "It's macho, I'm-the-law guys like you, Sheriff Hayden, that made me walk away from the Bureau. I think maybe the testosterone screws up your ability to see the obvious."

She cursed herself. She hadn't meant to say that. But she'd certainly hit his hot button with that one. A muscle flexed in his tense jaw and his nostrils flared. He was royally ticked. Alex felt oddly exhilarated by his reaction. Her heart pounded. Her pulse leapt. If verbal sparring with the man gave her this much of a rush, what would kissing him do for her? As if she'd stated the question out loud, his gaze dropped to her mouth. Her breath caught.

He was closer...Alex couldn't say whether she'd moved or he had, but she could feel his warm breath on her lips. Could feel the pull of his muscular body.

The door opened. They jumped apart. It was Peg.

"Sheriff, Roy, Willis and Dixon want to know if you're ready for their briefing?"

Mitch blinked away the spell he'd somehow fallen under. He felt disoriented. "Give me a minute, Peg." She nodded and turned away but not before he saw the question in her eyes. Peg hadn't missed the tension she'd interrupted.

"Is this about Miller and Saylor?" Alex demanded, drawing his reluctant attention back to her.

Mitch forced his wayward impulses back into submission. He'd almost kissed her. Would have kissed her if Peg hadn't interrupted. Damn. He couldn't let this crazy attraction get any more out of hand. She was a suspect and his only witness in this case. He had to get a grip. Not to mention that anyone outside his office who'd bothered to look would have seen them.

"This is about a lot of things. I'll have Peg call you in when we get to the part that concerns you." He looked anywhere but directly at her. He wasn't sure he could mask what she'd made him feel.

"We had a deal," she countered. "You're not supposed to leave me out."

Mitch rounded his desk and shuffled through the items stacked on the middle of his blotter. "I have something else for you to do in the meantime." He passed a large padded envelope to her. "These are the personal effects related to your investigation that were found in your rental car."

Slowly, as if wary of his motivation, she reached for the envelope. "Have you looked at them?"

His gaze fixed on hers. "No. Peg put it on my desk while we were out. I guess Forensics sent it over. You can tell me what you find." Mitch had reviewed the inventory list. Nothing the envelope contained grabbed his attention. Maybe allowing her to review the contents first would help him earn her trust. Besides, if the techs had found anything important they would have told him.

She stared at the envelope in her hands as if she feared it contained things she didn't want to know. "You can use Dixon's office." Mitch moved to her side and ushered her from his office. "Peg, show Ms. Preston to Dixon's office. She needs to do a little work without interruption."

"Yes, sir."

Mitch watched as Peg settled Alex at Dixon's desk. His chief deputy's office was directly across the reception area from Mitch's. Since all the inner walls of the offices were glass, he could keep an eye on Alex while he and his men conducted their briefing. And Dixon's office didn't have any windows facing the outside for Mitch to worry about. She should be safe there for a few minutes. Dixon, Willis and Roy, Mitch's cousin, sauntered out of the breakroom, coffee cups in hand.

"Let's get this done," Mitch said by way of invitation into his office.

"Where's that pretty P.I.?" Roy asked as he settled into one of the chairs in front of Mitch's desk.

Mitch took his own seat. "She's going over some material in Dixon's office."

All three of his deputies glanced toward the office in question. "When are you going to let one of us have a turn at guarding the little lady?" Willis wanted to know, his question dragging their reluctant gazes back to Mitch.

Irritation swelled inside him. "Tell me what you've got, Dixon." Mitch didn't bother to answer Willis's question, because he wasn't about to trust Alex's safety to anyone else. He squashed that little voice that taunted him with suggestions of ulterior motives. He had no ulterior motive. Just because he was physically attracted to her didn't mean anything. Hell, he was a man. What man alive wouldn't be attracted to her?

The next hour was spent going over every detail of what they knew so far regarding Miller's and Saylor's murders. The autopsy report on Jasna Bukovak was still not available. So they had nothing new on that front. Nothing but mounting evidence that pointed to Alex Preston. Evidence that made no sense, had no foundation and didn't quite connect.

"I want you to keep pounding the pavement," Mitch

instructed. "Someone had to see or hear something. An assassin didn't just walk into that hotel, kill one of my men and then walk out without encountering another human being."

"Should we put out an appeal for information on channel 6?" Dixon offered. "A reporter called this morning offering to do a special segment on the investigation."

"That's worked in the past for Davidson County," Willis added hopefully, clearly excited about the possibility of garnering his five minutes of fame.

"Let's not go down that road just yet," Mitch said, noting the letdown in both Willis's and Roy's eyes. "We don't want to let our man know just how little we've got at this point."

"What if our man is a woman?" Roy suggested.

All eyes shifted toward Dixon's office and the woman working there.

"I'm not ruling out anything at this point," Mitch said, pulling their attention back to him. "But until she remembers what happened, we'll just have to keep beating the bushes."

Peg, who had obviously been listening from her desk just outside the door, stuck her head into Mitch's office. "I have a suggestion, Sheriff."

"Let's hear it." Mitch motioned for her to enter. "Lord knows we've pretty much hit a dead end."

"Hypnosis," she said succinctly. "It worked for my husband."

She'd lost Mitch. "Hypnosis? What do you mean it worked for your husband?"

She braced her hands on her wide hips and looked at Mitch as if he should know what she was talking about. "You know my Ronnie used to smoke two packs of cigarettes a day," she reminded impatiently. "He got himself hypnotized and now he doesn't smoke. It was that simple."

"Hey, Peg," Dixon piped up, straightening in his chair. "That's a great idea. They do it in the movies when someone can't remember something. A few minutes under hypnosis and they remember everything, clear back to a former life."

"I think I saw that movie," Willis added, nodding his agreement.

"Can they really do that?" Roy looked as taken aback as Mitch felt.

"Sure they can," Peg insisted. "Dr. Letsen did my Ronnie's and it worked like a charm. Do you want me to call and make an appointment for her, Sheriff?"

The thought of someone messing with Alex's mind didn't sit too well with Mitch. "Let me think about that, Peg. I appreciate the suggestion."

"Letsen can help her remember. I'd bet money on it," Peg said adamantly before returning to her desk.

"She might be right," Dixon allowed. "We don't have anything to lose at this point."

"I said I'd think about it." Mitch immediately regretted his sharp tone. The three deputies stared in bewilderment or accusation at him now. Or hell, maybe it was his guilty conscience nagging at him. He'd let Alex get too close, let it get personal. And he knew better.

"Well." Dixon stood. "While you're thinking about that, we'll get back out there and see what we can find. I'm certain we'll get a break soon."

Willis and Roy got to their feet, as did Mitch. "Thanks, Dixon." Mitch hesitated a moment, then added, "Give Talkington a call. Ask him if he has checked into Gill's college days and any missing young women from the area where he attended school like that profiler suggested.''

Dixon looked more than a little confused at the abrupt subject change. ''All right, Sheriff. You think maybe the profiler was right about the killings in Davidson County not being his first?''

He couldn't say what possessed him to go along with Alex's theory when he hadn't necessarily agreed with the original profiler's, but somehow he did. Mitch hadn't considered Gill clever enough or his methods sophisticated enough to be a seasoned killer. But Alex obviously saw something Mitch didn't. ''Let's just say that I think the possibility is worth looking in to,'' he admitted.

Dixon shrugged. ''I'll give him a call.''

''I'll bet we find out he killed that Bukovak girl, too,'' Roy added sagely. ''That bastard's crazy as hell.''

Mitch definitely agreed with that summation. He just wished he could convince Alex.

''Hayden, there's something—'' Alex halted abruptly just inside Mitch's office door. ''I'm sorry. I didn't realize...'' Her words drifted off as she surveyed the expectant faces around her.

She'd obviously been too busy looking at the notebook in her hands to notice that his meeting hadn't ended.

''Alex Preston, I think you already know Deputy Russ Dixon,'' Mitch said.

She nodded.

''Ma'am.'' Dixon inclined his head in acknowledgement.

''Over here are Deputies Arlon Willis and Roy

Becker," Mitch continued. Willis, to Mitch's annoyance, only stood there without saying a word or nodding or anything, his mouth hanging open in abject awe, but Roy gave her a two-fingered salute.

Alex's attention paused on Roy. Several moments passed with her looking directly at him as if she were trying to decide if they'd met before. Mitch imagined that she suffered that uncertainty with most every new face she encountered.

"Thanks, gentlemen," Mitch announced, breaking the awkward tension resulting from Alex's continued stare. "We'll touch base again about this time tomorrow unless one of you comes up with something new between now and then."

Dixon merely grunted his agreement as he headed for the door. Alex stepped aside to allow the deputies to pass. Roy hesitated next to her.

"You're looking much better, Ms. Preston. If you're feeling up to any backtracking, let me know and I'll be glad to take you around to any place you think might help you remember what happened that night."

"Thank you, Deputy Becker." She smiled faintly. "I appreciate the offer."

"Thanks, Roy," Mitch ground out, unreasonably annoyed with his flirting.

"Anytime, Sheriff." Grinning, he winked then sauntered away.

"You found something," Mitch said when Alex continued to stand there and stare after Roy.

Her forehead scrunched in concentration, Alex crossed the office to stand in front of Mitch's desk. "He seems familiar to me," she said distractedly.

"I don't know how much you remember from that morning, but he and Willis are the ones who got to the scene first. Roy never left your side until the medics arrived.''

Alex frowned thoughtfully. ''That must be it.''

''What've you got there?'' Mitch asked, drawing her attention back to the reason she'd come into his office in the first place.

She blinked, then stared down at the notebook in her hands. ''This,'' she said finally. ''This is the casebook I kept on the Bukovak investigation.'' She lifted her gaze to his, confusion and worry reigning supreme in those amber eyes. ''I always keep one for every case I work. They're usually pretty complete. But several pages have been ripped out of this one.'' She flipped through the first few pages of the spiral notebook. ''And then I get to the afternoon before...before Miller's murder and something's wrong.''

Mitch tensed. Maybe he should have looked in that envelope first. There hadn't been any casebook listed on the inventory. Forensics didn't usually make mistakes like that. ''Oh yeah, and what would that be?''

She chewed that lower lip the way she always did when she was deep in thought. The gesture made Mitch want to reach out and touch those full lips, and then to smooth that frown line from her brow.

''I kept a detailed log of everyone I interviewed and of my meetings with Jasna.'' She looked up at Mitch again. ''I met with her that day. There's nothing here that would point to giving her reason to lose hope.'' Alex shook her head slowly from side to side. ''She wouldn't have killed herself like that. I know it. Someone wanted it to look like she'd committed suicide, that's all.''

Mitch blew out an impatient breath. ''So now we

have three murders and a missing person, is that your assessment?''

Certainty replaced all other emotion in her eyes. "Yes, it is."

"I have to have evidence. I can't operate on conjecture."

"Someone is trying to set me up," she said quietly. "Whoever it is, he wants it to look like I killed Miller, and he wants to make it look as though it had nothing to do with Marija's disappearance. It would be so easy considering Gill has killed a half-dozen young women we know of, and Jasna is dead, to just assume Marija was one of his victims. Whoever is doing this knows I can't prove that Marija was pregnant unless I find her."

"So you feel the real killer has gone to all these elaborate efforts to set you up all because you were trying to find Marija?" That just didn't sound feasible.

"That's right," Alex argued, obviously reading the disbelief and condescension in his tone. "Why else would someone take my notes? There are so many pages missing. It looks as if he went through and took the pages that would be the most incriminating."

Mitch laughed then. Now she was accusing someone of stealing select pages from her notes. Wouldn't it have been easier just to destroy the notebook altogether? "And just who would have the kind of motivation required to go to all this trouble to cover up one missing girl?"

"I can't answer that yet. Your uncle is the key player with the most to lose."

Mitch gritted his teeth to hold back the irritation that roared through him with that comment.

Those amber eyes locked with his. "Everything after

5:00 p.m. the day before I was found in Miller's car has been ripped out," she said, her tone deadpan. "But the last entry, the five o'clock entry, says I intended to pay you a visit. Did I come to your house that evening? Is that how I knew where you live?"

Chapter Six

Alex followed Hayden into the small market on the corner of Commerce and Main. He'd said he needed to pick up a few things if they planned to eat tonight. Though her appetite remained nonexistent, he didn't appear to have suffered any setbacks in his. She touched her forehead and tried yet again to remember what had taken place the night Miller was murdered. Nothing came beyond what she'd already recalled. A man wearing a black ski mask. The same man beating her unmercifully. She frowned at the remembered pain of slamming into the tree trunk that had sent her into oblivion that night.

The voice. She'd heard a man's voice, but no voice she'd heard since triggered any recognition.

Hayden's angry voice echoed in her ears. Somehow she kept getting the memories of heated words with him mixed up with whatever happened that night.

Alex studied her host and wondered again at his somewhat hesitant response to her question about whether or not she had spoken with him the evening before Miller's murder.

He'd admitted to their meeting. He'd even gone on to tell her that they had argued about her investigation into his uncle's personal life. She remembered clearly now that Sheriff Hayden had put the word out that no one should talk to her. And they hadn't. Alex had been furious. Their eventual confrontation had been vehement, though she still only remembered tiny snippets. According to Hayden, she had left in a huff and he hadn't seen her again until the next morning when he arrived at the crime scene.

"You have anything against spaghetti?" Hayden asked, interrupting her worrisome reverie.

"What?" Alex shook off the heavy thoughts and tried to focus on the sheriff. He'd taken a jar of spaghetti sauce from a shelf.

"We're having this tonight." He flashed the red sauce and a bag of pasta he'd picked up without her noticing. "Do you have a problem with it?"

"No. Sorry. I was…somewhere else. Spaghetti is fine." She had to stay focused, distraction was not a good thing right now. "As long as we have a salad to go with it," she qualified as an afterthought. "Do *you* have a problem with that?" she added, tossing his question back at him.

Hayden smiled, a slow-in-coming gesture that affected only one side of his mouth. If she'd thought him good-looking before, that smile sent him well beyond that description in her estimation. Her heart did a little tattoo and she had the wildest impulse to pull all that blond hair loose and run her fingers through it. Her breath caught at the foolish notion.

"No," he said in that deep, smooth voice that spoke of long, hot, southern nights and didn't help her composure at all. "In fact, I think it's a great idea. You can make it."

Alex couldn't prevent her own tiny smile. She

should have seen that one coming, but she'd been too preoccupied with his handsome face and his voice and all that sexy hair. "Point me in the direction of the produce department," she said before her mind could wander down another dangerous path.

"This way." He headed down the aisle. "I guess that means we'll have to agree on some sort of salad dressing."

There was no point in trying to figure him out, but she couldn't help herself. Was he being overly nice now because he felt guilty for their heated exchange the night Miller died? Or was he simply trying to make the best out of a bad situation? She supposed that he could just feel bad that she'd had such a lousy day. Her client was dead and a serial killer had attacked her. She was definitely having a bad week. With so many choices it would be difficult to select the lowest point since her arrival in Raleigh County. Dressing, she reminded herself. He'd mentioned dressing.

"As long as it's not French, I'll be happy." She hurried to keep up with his long strides.

That pulse-pumping smile eased into a half grin as they reached the main aisle that stretched across the back of the store. "And French is my favorite."

"Mitch?" A feminine voice called from a few feet away.

Alex looked toward the intrusion to find a woman of about fifty staring in their direction. Standing near a produce counter, she held a celery stalk in her hand, her shopping cart laden with the other selections she'd already made.

Hayden walked straight up to her and gifted her with a light peck on the cheek. "How's my favorite lady?"

The instant and fierce pang of jealousy Alex experienced was totally ridiculous. But she felt it anyway.

The woman who'd lifted her cheek so readily to Hayden stiffened when her gaze collided with Alex's. "Is that…?" Her words trailed off as if the rest were too unspeakable to utter.

Alex felt a twinge of trepidation.

"Alex Preston, this is my aunt Nadine," Hayden said, hesitation slowing him as he spoke. "Nadine Malloy," he added when Alex still looked puzzled.

Phillip's wife. She remembered now. The woman who'd opened her home to Marija. "Hello, Mrs. Malloy." Alex offered her hand.

Nadine glared at her. "You stay away from my family."

She'd obviously already heard what Alex had been up to before she'd gotten the knock on the head. "I'm only trying to find out what happened to Marija," Alex explained.

Hatred filled the woman's eyes. "We took that girl in and treated her like she was our own. Don't you dare come here accusing my husband and me of anything bad. I won't stand for it. If something happened to that girl after she left our home it had nothing to do with us."

Alex instinctively moved back a step from Nadine's fury. "Then you should be glad that I'm trying to find the truth. Otherwise there will always be suspicion connected to your family."

The woman advanced the step Alex had retreated. "The only person casting suspicion is you. If you know what's good—"

"Nadine." Mitch moved between the two of them. "You don't want to do this."

"She's done nothing but cause pain and loss since she came to this town," Nadine said coldly. "How can you defend her?"

Mitch knew his unusual treatment of this case—of Alex—was cause for dissension in his family. They felt betrayed, and he understood. But he had to do what he had to do. The realization that he was hurting the people he cared most about for a stranger stabbed deep into his chest.

"It's my job to see after her until she regains her memory and we can find out who killed Miller and Saylor. If I don't do this we might never know." Mitch knew Alex was listening to and analyzing every word that he said. This little episode would damage the flimsy trust that had started to build between them, but that couldn't be helped. Nadine was family. He couldn't turn his back on family.

Nadine shook the celery stalk at Alex. "You already have your murderer," she said cruelly. "She should be locked up in a cell not walking around free."

He heard Alex's sharp intake of breath and he wanted to turn to her…to somehow comfort the hurt he knew that comment had dealt her.

"Let it go for now, Nadine," Mitch warned softly. "Let's not make a scene."

As if suddenly realizing where she was, Nadine stepped back. "I'm sorry, Mitch." She turned a watery gaze up to him. "This isn't your fault. Of course you're doing the best job you can. You'll figure this all out and then things can go back to the way they used to be." She speared one last withering look in Alex's direction. "Before she came to town."

Nadine pitched the celery back onto the produce shelf and rushed away with her grocery cart. Mitch hoped this business wasn't going to push her back into another bout of depression. She'd suffered with periods of severe depression for so long, but the last couple of years had been better. Mitch didn't want to be the cause of a relapse. He let go a mighty breath and turned back to Alex.

She opened her mouth to speak, but he cut her off. "Don't talk. Let's just get what we need and get out of here."

EVERYTHING ABOUT this investigation stunk, Mitch ruminated as he drove toward home. Two good men were dead. His aunt and uncle were devastated by the innuendos obviously floating around. And he wanted nothing more than to console Alex for his aunt's behavior. It was nuts. Alex was the enemy. A suspect, a witness. The very person poised to do his family harm. The woman who'd betrayed his trust, if only for a few hours that night. The one who seemed to have set all this chaos into motion. Yet he wanted to protect her, to keep her safe and happy as if she meant a great deal more to him than...

Who was he kidding? She did mean a great deal more to him than she should. Mitch shook his head in defeat. He'd completely lost his perspective. How in the hell was he supposed to be objective when all he could think about was...sex? Having sex with Alex. He'd pretended it was her well-being he was concerned about when actually it was her, plain and simple.

He wanted her. She challenged him on a level that no other woman had. Though he'd had his share of relationships, none ever stuck. He'd never met a woman who could match him on the job. Until now that is. Simply sharing a conversation with her had aroused more than his intellectual interest. He stole a glance at his passenger. The tiny bandage on her forehead and the mark on her cheek made her look vulnerable, but Mitch knew she wasn't. Not really. She was tough and smart. She clearly knew as much about the law and investigating crime as he did. And there was something intensely erotic about a woman who could hold her own with him. A woman who knew too much about him before she ever met him.

Today, when she'd spouted off all that she knew about him, he'd been startled. He wondered if she had remembered their dinner together. Not that he'd said those things to her in quite that way. If she had remembered, it definitely had not affected her the way it had him.

Mitch cursed himself.

Alex Preston was far from the kind of woman Mitch hoped to settle down with someday. His father had found a special kind of woman in Mitch's mother. A woman who loved her husband and family fiercely and gave up her career to dedicate herself to that family. Though Alex represented in every way the kind of woman with whom he longed to share a physical relationship, she was not the type who would give up her fancy city job to be a country mother and housewife. She was too focused on doing whatever it took to accomplish her mission. Even lying to him.

And Mitch wasn't going down the matrimony road with that kind of woman. He'd watched his brother's life fall apart because of conflicting goals and interests. Mitch had no intention of following that path.

As he turned onto the gravel drive that would lead to his house he considered the direction his thoughts had taken. Alex was in his custody—part of a case—

and here he was analyzing why they couldn't spend their lives together.

Damn, but he was really losing it. Maybe she wasn't the only one who'd had her brains scrambled. Or maybe Roy was right, Mitch just needed to jump-start his social life. Roy had been urging Mitch to get back into the nightlife scene for months. But he'd worked too many hours this past year and didn't see that routine changing anytime soon.

Mitch parked the Jeep in front of his house and made a decision. From this moment on he would not think of Alex as a woman. She was a suspect, a witness, part of an ongoing case. He didn't have time for a social life. Especially not until this case was resolved.

"Unless you're in a hurry for that salad," Alex said, jerking him back to the present, "I'd like to take a long hot bath. I'm beat."

The image of her naked body, all long legs and curves, lounging in a tub filled with hot water and frothy bubbles filled his mind. His entire body reacted instantly, going rock hard. "Sure," he croaked. "Take your time. I'll make the salad." The last thing he needed right now was Alex in the kitchen with him trying to help.

He needed distance to get his act together.

HAYDEN BARELY SPOKE to her during dinner. He rushed through the meal and into his study as if being in the same room with her made him ill somehow. Alex guessed it was because of his aunt's reaction to his taking Alex in.

Flipping her freshly washed hair over her shoulders, she turned and retraced her steps across the kitchen. She supposed Nadine was right to some extent. Things had gone down hill since Alex came to town. Marija was still missing. Jasna was dead. Two deputies had lost their lives. She pressed her hand against her waist when her stomach knotted with a mixture of fear and regret.

She muttered a curse and pivoted on her heel. Why couldn't she remember what happened that night? Or anytime since her arrival in Shady Grove? She needed to figure this out. Whoever had done these horrible things couldn't be allowed to get away with it. Her casebook had helped. She knew when she read the entries that they were correct. She had done those things. She could remember them in a strange kind of way. Sort of like when her grandmother told her things she did as a child. Although Alex had no actual memory of doing them, it felt right, like her brain somehow knew she had done them whether she could recall the acts or not.

But this was much, much worse than not recalling a childhood caper. A murderer was going to go free if she couldn't remember these incidents. Instinct told her that he, whoever he was, intended to take her out of the picture just to be sure she didn't ruin his perfect crime spree. A shiver raced up Alex's spine. How could she not remember the face of the man who wanted her dead? Who was determined to make it look as if she had committed murder? The ski mask flashed, leaving no hope of remembering his face. But the eyes. She should remember the eyes. His size. His voice. Surely, she could recall those things. She did remember one voice but it didn't seem to belong to the man in the mask.

"Dammit."

She plowed her fingers through her hair and mas-

saged her skull. Thankfully, her head didn't hurt anymore. She'd exchanged the bandage on her forehead
for a couple of Band-Aids. The bruise and Waylon
Gill's handiwork were almost gone from her cheek
she'd noticed while drying her hair tonight. She still
sported a few scratches and bruises on her back and
side. But the worst of the soreness was gone. And her
scraped knees were healing nicely.

If only her memory would heal as quickly.

"Think, Alex," she demanded crossly as she pressed
her fingertips to her temples. "What did you see?"

Nothing came.

"This is ridiculous." She stalked over to the sink
and leaned against the counter to stare out at the night.
Why couldn't she recall just one more thing from that
other night? It had been dark, just like now. She'd been
in an unfamiliar environment—also like now. Alex
closed her eyes and strained to remember just one
thing. Nothing.

She snapped her eyes open and swore. She had to
do something to occupy herself or she would surely go
nuts. Hayden was doing paperwork and didn't want to
be disturbed. She had no interest in television or reading. She could only replay the day's events like some
kind of twisted short film. The evil in Gill's eyes. The
fear she'd felt when he attacked her. Jasna's lifeless,
unblinking gaze.

Enough.

She glanced over her shoulder at the casebook lying
open on the table. She'd been over it and over it, but
too many strategic pages were missing.

The cool autumn breeze wafted through the open
window momentarily drawing Alex from her troubling
thoughts. She inhaled deeply. This was the one good

thing about living in the country. Everything smelled so fresh.

A flapping sound startled her. Alex jumped back from the counter. It came again. She frowned and inched back toward the counter. She leaned over the sink and peered out the window. It was too dark to see anything, just vague outlines. The noise seemed connected to the breeze, whenever it kicked up the flapping started again.

Curious now, she padded quietly to the back door and stared through the glass panes. She still couldn't see anything. Alex moistened her lips and flipped the switch for the porch light. A yellow haze of light spilled over the wooden porch casting the yard beyond it in eerie shadows.

Alex studied the items on the porch for a moment. A couple of old rockers, and on the far side of the porch stood a metal garbage can, the lid haphazardly pressed over the top of it. It wasn't the old beat-up can itself that caught Alex's eye, but a piece of paper flapping in the late September breeze. The page was one torn from a spiral notebook, one edge ragged. The same kind of notebook she used to record the details of a case. The same casebook she now had with missing pages.

Her gaze never leaving the fluttering piece of paper, Alex unlatched the screen door and moved across the porch toward the can. Her heart pounding, her hand shaking, she reached for the trapped paper. She tugged it loose and turned it right side up so she could read the words written there.

Tuesday, September 3rd, 7:30 p.m., meeting with Deputy Miller.

"Oh, God."

Alex pushed the lid off the can and a couple more loose pages flapped like the wings of birds just released from their cage. Alex grabbed the pages. Both displayed her handwriting. She shook her head in denial. Mitch Hayden had lied to her. He had taken those pages. He had...

Her breath fled her lungs.

What else had he lied to her about?

The pages slipped from her suddenly lax hands and drifted off the porch to the grass, flipping end over end out of her reach. Startled into action to save her notes, Alex rushed down the steps into the darkness. She snatched up one page, rushed the few feet to the next and reached for it.

A strong hand clamped down over her mouth. An arm belted around her waist. Panic exploded inside her chest.

Alex tried to scream but the sound died in her throat.

Her assailant jerked her against his body. She had to get away. He held her tighter. She felt the scratch of his wool ski mask. She dug her heels in trying to slow his movements as he dragged her toward the woods beyond the yard. Terror roared through her veins.

She had to stop him!

She kicked backward, aiming for his shins. She connected. He grunted. She slammed her left elbow into his abdomen, and kicked again. He growled a savage sound. Alex twisted violently, kicking and flailing her arms. She bit down on his hand with all her might.

She was free!

She scrambled to her feet and ran screaming toward

the house. Her lungs burned for oxygen. She had to move faster. She slammed head-on into a hard body. She jerked back. She had to run. He reached for her. She pivoted from his grasp.

Run! her brain commanded.

Strong arms locked around her waist. She hit the ground, kicking and screaming.

"Stop fighting dammit! It's me."

Hayden. Alex stilled, her breath shuddering in and out. Her chest burned for more air. Her entire body trembled as the adrenaline receded leaving only the fear.

"It's okay." He murmured soothingly. "Let's get you in the house."

Trembling so savagely she could hardly move, she allowed him to pull her to her feet. The unsteadiness of her limbs forced her to lean on him as he ushered her back into the house. She sank into a ladderback chair the instant she reached the table. She closed her eyes and tried to calm her racing heart. Her body strummed with fear. Every place her assailant had touched stung with the remnants of terror still plaguing her. He'd almost gotten her. Then she would be dead just like Jasna.

She clamped her hand over her mouth and stifled a sob. She remembered Jasna's worry for her sister, her tearful gratitude when the agency accepted her case. And now she was gone.

"What the hell happened?" Hayden locked the door and slid into a chair next to her. "What were you doing outside?"

She swallowed and tried to moisten her dry lips, but her mouth was too parched. Her mind was whirling with too many images and sensations. "It was him. He tried to…'' She closed her eyes and sucked in another quaking breath. She searched for calm, tried to imagine it embracing her. "I found the—" Her gaze collided with his.

The pages.

The pages she needed to retrace her steps. Pages he had stolen and then tried to destroy.

"You," she whispered. She bolted out of her chair, overturning it in her haste. "It was you who stole my notes."

Mitch stood, bewildered by her words. "What the hell are you talking about?"

"They were in your trash can," she said as she backed away from him. "That's why I went out onto the porch. And then he came out of nowhere and grabbed me. Or maybe it was you."

What the hell was she accusing him of? Her screams had brought Mitch running. He'd raced out of the house to find her flying across the yard as if the devil himself was on her heels, but he hadn't seen anyone. Then he'd considered that maybe she had regained some memory that sent her into the darkness then frightened her, like at the clearing.

The rest of what she'd said sank in. How could she have found her notes in his trash can? "What notes? The notes you claimed are missing from your notebook?"

Alex looked at her hands as if she expected the pages to be there. She frowned. "I must have dropped them outside."

He tried to think if he'd seen anything besides her out there. He hadn't. He'd been so intent on getting to her all else had kind of faded into insignificance.

She took a step toward the door, then stalled.

"They're out there." She pointed to the back door, her gaze narrowing with suspicion. "You should know. You had to be the one to steal them."

"This is ridiculous. I told you I didn't even look in the envelope before I gave it to you. I didn't know you had a casebook."

"Then how did the pages get out there?"

She was accusing him of attempting to destroy evidence. He reached beneath his shirt and removed his handgun. He'd tucked it there and raced out of the house when he'd heard her scream.

She gasped.

Mitch glared at her. Did she think he was going to shoot her now as well? "Don't move," he commanded.

Furious with himself and with her, he jerked the door open and stalked out to the trash can. He surveyed his backyard and found nothing. No intruder. No papers. The trash can's lid was on the ground next to the porch. Mitch surveyed the can and saw nothing but the closed white plastic bags he used to store his trash. He scanned the yard once more before going back inside.

She waited expectantly on the other side of the room.

He locked the door and faced her. "There's nothing out there."

She shook her head. "That's not possible." She started forward again. "I know what I saw." She displayed her empty palms. "I held them in my hands."

"Well, they're gone now." Mitch massaged the back of his neck. God, he was tired. He didn't have the energy to deal with this tonight. "I don't know what you saw or what you think you saw, but nothing's there now, so let's just call it a night."

"I'm not staying here." She backed away a few

steps. "I can't trust you. I know what I saw," she repeated.

Mitch swore hotly under his breath. If he moved in too aggressively, she'd make a run for it. He couldn't let her do that since she was in his custody and on the off chance that there was any truth to what she said about being attacked. Though he doubted it, considering what she'd said about the missing pages of her notes. He didn't have them. She had to have imagined the episode. Calling the neurologist would be tomorrow's first order of business.

"Where would you like to go?" he asked carefully, taking a half step in her direction. "Back to the hospital…or maybe to a cell?"

"Don't patronize me, Hayden." She fell back the half step he'd taken. "I don't know what you're hiding."

"I'm not hiding anything." He moved closer. "You have two choices here, Alex. You can either trust me or you can take up residence in a cell until we've determined the threat to you and your involvement in these homicides."

"How can you expect me to trust you now?" One more step brought her up against the wall. Panic widened those amber eyes. "I'm…confused. The pages were there. I saw them. You had to have put them there."

He closed in on her fully now, trapping her between the wall and his body. "If I'd wanted to hurt you, I would have done so while you were sleeping last night or the night before. You have to know you're safe here. We'll figure this out in the morning. But right now you need to relax. You can trust me. I didn't take those pages."

She held up her right hand to ward him off. "I...I don't know, Hayden."

A fresh set of scratches on the inner side of her right forearm snagged Mitch's attention. "What's this?" He grabbed her wrist and turned her arm up for his inspection. She tried to pull loose but Mitch held her firmly.

"When he grabbed me I struggled. I guess he scratched me when I broke free."

Mitch muttered a four-letter word. Unless she'd scratched herself and that didn't look like the case, someone else had. Adrenaline sent his heart pounding. His grip tightened on her wrist. "Don't ever go outside again unless I'm with you."

"Does that mean you believe me now?"

"I don't know what I believe but I'm not taking any chances."

"And the pages from my casebook? My notes?"

He held her gaze, worry twisting inside him. This was too close. Way too close. "Maybe the pages were bait?"

She looked startled. "I wouldn't have gone out if I hadn't seen the pages."

Mitch couldn't decide which he wanted to do most, take care of her or go outside and hunt down the bastard who'd hurt her. But he wouldn't risk leaving her alone. "Come on, let's put something on those scratches."

She still seemed a little reluctant, but she followed him anyway. Mitch reached into the medicine cabinet and retrieved the things he would need to take care of her latest injuries. She lingered in the doorway, as if afraid to get trapped in such a small space with him.

He crooked his finger at her. "Come here."

An unsteady breath heaved past her lips. He hated that she was afraid of him. If she ever remembered what he said to her that night… He swore. That would not be a good thing considering their precarious bond at the moment. Finally, she moved toward him, at once brave and vulnerable, and making him all the more aware of his fierce desire to protect her. A desire that went way beyond the call of duty.

She paused less than two feet away and extended her arm.

Using a cotton ball and antiseptic he swabbed the scratches. She winced against the sting.

"Sorry," he murmured. He drew her arm closer and blew to relieve the sting.

She watched him, her gaze drifting up to meet his.

The smoothness of her skin beneath his fingers tugged at his senses, made him want to touch more of her. Made him want to press his lips there. The needy look in her eyes only made him want her more. Forcing his attention to the task at hand, he swabbed the antibiotic ointment on next.

"That should do it," he said tautly, still holding on to her.

"Thank you."

The lingering uncertainty in her eyes made him ache to show her in whatever way it took that she could trust him. Unable to resist the temptation, he reached up with his free hand and traced the fading mark from her encounter with Gill. She shivered but didn't draw away. He still wanted to kill the guy for touching her.

"I don't know, Preston," he murmured. "I can't decide if you're just incredibly brave or completely reckless."

She smiled, just the tiniest gesture. "After tonight, I

think I'd have to say a little of both.'' Worry still haunted her amber gaze.

''You really think I stole your notes and was dumb enough to stash 'em in my trash can?'' He caressed the sensitive side of her wrist with his thumb. Slow little circles. The feel of her skin made him ache. He was treading on thin ice here.

She closed her eyes and sighed. ''I don't know what I think.'' After a moment she opened that soft, warm gaze to his once more. ''I only know that someone wants me out of the picture and I wish I knew why.''

''Don't worry, I won't let this happen again. From now on, you don't make a move without me.''

''That might be a little tricky,'' she suggested, the smile reaching her eyes this time. ''Unless, of course, you're planning to ask me to sleep with you.''

''Do you want me to ask?''

She held his gaze for a second or two before she answered. He could see the battle taking place in her eyes. It was the same one he struggled with.

''I don't want to complicate things,'' she said softly. ''Especially not now.''

''You mean since you have reason to suspect me.''

She turned her palm into his, allowing him to hold her hand, showing her fledgling trust. ''I mean since I don't know what's going on up here.'' She tapped her temple. ''I'm not thinking clearly.''

''I guess I'll have to take the chair then.''

She moistened her lips and gifted him with another of those fragile smiles. ''As strange as it sounds after what I thought a few minutes ago, I'd feel a lot safer with you close by.'' She shrugged. ''I don't know what it is about you.'' She traced the pattern of the star he wore on his left shirt pocket. "Maybe it's because you're the sheriff. You know, one of the good guys."

"I'll take that as a compliment."

He resisted the urge to hold on to her hand when she turned away.

"There's just one thing," he said, giving her pause.

She looked back expectantly.

Mitch cupped her cheeks and drew her close for the very briefest meeting of the lips. He couldn't say exactly what possessed him at that moment. He just had to do it. He had to taste her. To feel her lips beneath his. And she tasted every bit as refreshingly sweet as he'd known she would. Her mouth felt marvelously soft and vulnerable beneath his. He wanted to get lost in her more than he'd ever wanted to do anything in his life.

His body hardened instantly. And in that moment he knew that kissing her would never be enough. But right now, she needed to be kissed. And so did he. He'd missed out on kissing her that first time, but not tonight. Tonight he followed his heart, as foolish as that likely was.

She drew back first, breathless, her face flushed. She licked her lips, tasting their kiss. "I'll just go get ready for bed now."

"I'll be there in a minute." Mitch watched her go, already berating himself for allowing that kiss, and for knowing that it would never, ever be enough. One thing was certain, he had to regain control before he set foot in that bedroom. The image of her lying amid a mound of rumpled sheets in nothing but a skimpy T-shirt...

The ringing of the telephone shattered the arousing picture.

Shaken more by the kiss than he had anticipated, Mitch strode to the living room and snatched up the receiver. "Hayden."

"Talkington here, Hayden."

Mitch frowned. He glanced at his watch, it was late. "What's up, Talkington?"

"Well, it looks like we've found another of Gill's victims. I'm in the middle of the woods right now. It's going to be morning before we have anything to look at. I just thought you'd want to know. Could be your missing girl, I suppose. Looks as if she's been here long enough to be the one you're looking for."

"Marija Bukovak?" Mitch asked knowing full well who Talkington meant.

"Can't tell yet. I'll give you a call as soon as we know something."

Chapter Seven

Alex jerked awake. Her fingers fisted in the sheets as the final remnants of her erotic dream faded, leaving her hot and aching. She closed her eyes and drew in a deep breath. Man, that had been too real. Her lids drifted open as the images from her dream clicked past, frame by frame. Mitch smiling down at her. The warmth flowing between them, drawing her nearer when she was already far too close. His opening her car door...

The gray sedan.

She sat up, drawing her knees to her chest. The gray sedan was her rental car. The one that had been towed away as evidence. She closed her eyes and relived emerging from that same vehicle at the clearing the night Miller was murdered.

Did that mean that her dream was real? Was there some other connection between her and Mitch? She frowned. When had she started calling him Mitch?

Remembering the promise he'd made to stay close by, she turned to the large upholstered chair that sat to the left of her night table. The soft, warm glow from the lamp lit his features. Mitch Hayden's eyes were closed in sleep. Long strands of tawny hair had worked loose from their leather tie and fell around his broad shoulders. The holster and weapon he wore beneath the loose chambray shirt made her feel safe. His long legs were outstretched in front of him. She wondered how he could possibly be comfortable in that chair?

Her gaze drifted back up to the weapon he carried. For the first time since all this began she wished she had her own weapon back. But it was evidence now. Alex shook her head to deny the reality that Miller had been killed with her weapon. Her prints were on it…but she hadn't made the deadly shot. She knew it deep in her heart. Whatever she had gone to that clearing to talk to him about, she had not killed him. Her intentions, if recorded, as far as Miller was concerned were among the missing pages. The pages she had seen tonight. She closed her eyes. God, how was she supposed to know what was real and what wasn't? Had she imagined the whole episode in Mitch's backyard? She thought of the scratches on her arm and consoled herself in the knowledge that she had proof of the attack.

But what about the pages?

The image of Mitch's gorgeous smile crept back into her thoughts and a flush of heat warmed her, chasing away those other fears and insecurities. Alex turned back to study her sleeping protector once more. Had something happened between them? Something besides the argument he had confessed to? Something…intimate?

Alex pushed the covers back and dropped her feet to the floor. She sat on the edge of the bed like that for a long time, just watching him, remembering his smile, his touch, the sound of his voice. Her fingers itched to trace the lean angular features of that handsome face. The square line of his jaw, the fullness of his lips, and that tiny cleft in his chin. Her gaze slid lower, along his neck and down the well-defined contours of his chest beneath the form-fitting T-shirt. The snug, worn soft jeans molded to his lean waist, well-defined masculine bulge and muscular thighs. The mismatched sweat socks made her smile.

"Can't sleep?"

The sound of his deep, sultry voice jerked her attention back up to his face. Those clear blue eyes looked straight into her soul, eliminating any possibility of denying what she felt just then.

"I had a dream," she admitted. "About you."

He leaned forward, bracing his elbows on his spread knees, and making her breath catch at his nearness. "Oh, yeah?"

She nodded, her throat so tight she wasn't sure she could speak. "When I woke up you were here. As if I'd somehow conjured you up from my imagination."

He inclined his head, taking his time to study every facet of her face as she had done his only moments ago. "Were we fighting in this dream?"

She shook her head.

The desire that flamed to life in his eyes made her heart pound like a drum in her chest. Instinctively, she moistened her lips in anticipation of his taste...of the feel of his lips against hers. He followed the movement, his expression so intent it made her tremble.

The renewed ache that welled inside her when he looked deeply into her eyes was a physical pain. She wanted to tell him that her dream was real...it had to be, no dream could feel like this one had, but she was afraid of breaking the spell that held them in this special cocoon of warmth and yearning. Nothing else could touch them here. Nothing else mattered.

"You were smiling at me," she said when she could no longer bear the tension filled silence. "You walked me to my car. It felt so real."

Something in his eyes changed, the shift so subtle she couldn't decipher it. Sadness...maybe.

"It was real."

Had she hurt him somehow? In some way besides the investigation into his uncle's life. The idea twisted inside her like barbed wire, made her want to reach out to him and make it all go away.

She chewed her lower lip, concentrating hard to remember every moment of the dream. She lifted her gaze back to his. "You didn't kiss me that night?"

"No."

And she knew in that instant what she wanted. Making her move from the bed before she had time to think about it and change her mind, she knelt in front of him and peered up into his eyes. This close she could smell his clean, masculine scent, could feel the warmth of his strong body.

The need she saw in his eyes made her dizzy. She braced her hands on his thighs to steady herself, reveling in the feel of hard muscle.

"Did something happen between us that I haven't remembered yet?" she asked, her voice as uneven as her equilibrium.

"Not what you think," he murmured, regret heavy in his husky voice.

Alex squeezed her eyes shut for a moment, trying to banish the funnel of feelings whirling inside her. He touched her. She caught her breath. Just the merest grazing of her cheek with his fingertips and then it was gone.

She opened her eyes to him and the battle was over. She was too weak to fight, too needy to think. She reached up and cupped his face in her hands. The barest hint of stubble scraped her palms. Slowly, giving him adequate time to stop her since she couldn't possibly stop herself, she lifted her mouth to his. Her whole body sighed as her lips brushed his.

His hands threaded into her hair, as if he might take control of the moment but he held back, his lips so close she could feel their pull, but not quite close enough to touch.

He inhaled deeply, drawing in their commingled breath. He opened his mouth as if to speak, but thought better of it and sealed his mouth over hers instead.

His kiss was slow, thorough and deep. It went on and on until she was gasping for air. When he at last drew back, his ragged breath fanned her lips making them burn for more of him. She buried her fingers in his thick hair and dragged it loose, then leaned back to admire him, but he had other plans. He pulled her mouth back up to his and nipped her lower lip with his teeth. His tongue slid along the seam of her lips and she opened. He invaded her so completely, closed his arms around her and held her so tightly against him that she felt a part of him, no longer separate.

Her fingers found their way to his shirt. She peeled it off those broad shoulders. He stood then, pulling her up with him. She felt his weight shift from one foot to the other as he toed off his socks. She pushed the shirt down his arms until it dropped to the floor. The shoulder holster went next. His hands and lips left her long enough for him to shed his T-shirt. Alex gasped when her palms flattened on his bare chest. She smoothed her hands over that sculpted terrain, learning every square inch of him. The sparse blond hair sprinkled there created a delicious friction. He was so beautifully made.

He caught the hem of her T-shirt and dragged it up and over her head, baring her body to him save for the skimpy panties that did little to conceal the part of her that ached so fiercely for him. The look of awe he wore gave her the courage to hold still until he'd had his fill of looking. Slowly, as if he feared she would bolt and run, he reached for her. His hand closed over her breast. Her eyes drifted shut and she allowed the sensations to wash over her. She felt the brush of his hair just before his mouth covered her taut nipple.

He sucked hard. She cried out. Dropping to his knees, he turned his attention to her other breast, licking, nibbling and sucking until she thought she would lose her mind. Her fingers speared into his silky hair and encouraged him.

He dragged her panties down her legs as his skillful mouth made a path down her abdomen. He teased her belly button with his tongue, while his hands glided up her thighs, over her rib cage, then traced down the length of her spine until those magic fingers taunted the sensitive cleft of her buttocks. Alex gasped. She threw back her head and cried out when his mouth moved lower still. He ushered her back onto the edge of the bed, his hands and his mouth never leaving her body.

Her whole being throbbed in time to the dance of a distant crescendo of sensations. He tasted her intimately, greedily. She moaned loud and long, her fingers fisting in the rumpled sheets. With every stroke of his tongue she edged closer and closer to the climax already sending little ripples along her feminine walls. He squeezed her buttocks, his tongue going deeper inside her.

She came hard and fast.

While the quakes of completion still rocked through her, he kissed his way back up her torso, lingering in all the right places. Weak from the explosion of senses, she fumbled for the closure to his jeans, desperate to touch him. He was looming over her now, half on, half off the bed, his mouth still torturing her breasts.

She eased the zipper down and pushed her hands inside his jeans. He was incredibly hard, smooth and pulsing. Her fingers molded around him, making her ache to have him inside her. Unable to wait, she shoved his jeans and briefs down over his hips at the same time that he planted a trail of kisses up the column of her throat. Using one foot, she pushed his jeans to his ankles.

She stroked the length of him. He groaned and drew away from the sensitive flesh he'd been plundering. He looked directly into her eyes, then he kissed her hard on the mouth. His tongue plunged into her mouth, filling her with the taste of hot sex and fierce male hunger. He wrapped one hand around her waist and pulled her against him as if she weighed nothing at all. The feel of his thick, satiny arousal against her tingling feminine flesh made her shiver. He climbed onto the bed, bringing her up to the mound of pillows. He placed her there as carefully as if she were of the most fragile glass, then kicked his jeans the rest of the way off.

Those blue eyes were alive with light and he worshiped her with that brilliant gaze. He kissed her chin, her nose and then each closed lid. When she opened her eyes to him again he held her gaze, his own fiery with desire. He kneed her thighs apart and positioned himself there. His tip nudged her. She arched into him, wanting. When he held back she grabbed him by the waist and tried to pull him to her. Still he resisted. She started to protest, but he silenced her with his mouth, kissing her until she whimpered with renewed need.

Finally, dear God, finally, he sank slowly, so very, very slowly into her. The drag of his male hardness along her supersensitive feminine walls produced an instant explosion. He held her body still with his own when she wanted to squirm and buck beneath him. The flood of sensations this time was overpowering, mind-blowing. She couldn't think. She couldn't breathe. She could only feel.

The rhythm began too slowly, and not until every last ripple of fulfillment had subsided within her. She wanted to scream. She needed to touch him. To feel every part of him. Her legs instinctively wrapped around his and her palms molded to his awesome chest. Her nipples stung with the pleasure he had wrought upon them and the anticipated feel of his bare flesh against those jutting peaks. Her body felt at once sated and needy. She couldn't get enough of him. She wanted more, and then some more after that.

She tried hard to focus on the feel of his skin, the intent expression on his face, but it was no use. He was pulling her into that vortex of pure sensation all over again with his rhythmic pumping. His pace increased, she felt him pulse inside her. His fingers fisted in the pillow on either side of her head as climax roared through him, drawing yet another one from her. She screamed with the strength of it. He kissed her, drinking in her cry of release.

Long minutes later, when their breathing had slowed, he held her close. Their skin was slick with perspiration. Neither of them spoke. There were no words that could adequately describe what they had just shared.

Even after the intense emotions and sensations were long gone, Alex knew deep in her heart that she had not made a mistake.

Making love with Mitch Hayden could never be considered a mistake. She snuggled closer to him and closed her eyes, at last allowing the clawing exhaustion to take her.

DAWN BROUGHT reality crashing down around Mitch.

God Almighty, what had he done?

He pressed his forehead against the cool tile wall and allowed the spray of water to flow over his back. What the hell had he done? He'd lost control and had sex with Alex. A suspect...a witness. He swore. And what made it worse was that it hadn't been just sex. He'd made love to her. Touched her the way he'd yearned to since the first time he laid eyes on her. Then he'd held her in his arms for the rest of the night. Held her close to his heart.

He was a fool.

He straightened and scrubbed the water and wet hair from his face. After slipping from her bed this morning, he'd sat for almost an hour and simply looked at her. Her silky black hair was fanned over her pillow. Her satiny thighs, creamy shoulders and delicate arms bared by the rumpled sheet that covered nothing but her torso and hips. Those lush, apple-red lips were swollen by his kisses.

He grew aroused at just the thought of her welcoming body. Mitch forced himself to put those thoughts out of his head and to go through the ritual of cleansing. He had to get his head on straight here. Talkington had another body. Mitch couldn't be sure what made him believe it might be the Bukovak girl, but Talkington wouldn't have mentioned her if he hadn't thought the possibility a strong one. Mitch didn't look forward to telling Alex. She was so sure that Gill had nothing to do with the girl's disappearance.

His lawman instincts warned him not to take Alex's conclusions too lightly.

But, he reminded himself, the facts would speak for themselves. Dental records would identify the girl. With the Bukovak girl's records readily available since she was already listed as missing, it wouldn't take long to find out one way or another.

Mitch stepped out of the shower and hastily dried himself off. He looped the towel around his waist and decided to forego a shave this morning. He was already running late.

"Good morning."

Alex stood propped in the open doorway watching him with blatant interest. She looked as if she'd been there awhile. She also looked as sexy as hell wearing his shirt and, from all appearances, nothing else.

"Morning."

"Mind if I shower next?"

He sidestepped, clearing the way for her. "Not at all." Maybe he'd shave after all.

While she grabbed a towel and hung it over the shower door, he wiped the steam from the mirror. He watched her lithe movements in the sweating glass. Memories of touching her and tasting her flicked in rapid succession in his mind. She shucked the shirt and he stilled. Seeing her slender body made him ache with renewed need, but the slowly fading bruises on her back enraged him. The idea of someone hurting her made him want to tear something apart with his bare hands. She stepped into the shower and closed the door. He squeezed his eyes shut and released a labored breath.

The sound of the water running forced his eyes open and his attention back to his reflection. The man staring back at him wasn't as smart as he should be. He damned well wasn't thinking straight, that was for sure. But, one way or another, whether he ever solved this case, he would not allow anyone to hurt Alex again. If anyone tried, he'd make sure it was the last thing he ever did.

MITCH STRUGGLED to keep his attention on the briefing Dixon presented. They still didn't have anything. Both Miller's and Alex's cars were clean. Except for the drugs, there was nothing out of the ordinary at all. And no prints, other than Miller's and Alex's. There was an extra set of tire tracks at the scene that didn't belong to either of their vehicles, but the particular type of tires was far too common to be of any real assistance.

Talkington was going to call Mitch as soon as he had determined if the Jane Doe they'd found was Marija Bukovak. He had opted not to tell Alex until he knew for sure.

Leaning back in his chair, he glanced toward Dixon's office where Alex was talking with a waitress who'd served Alex at the diner on several occasions. Her name had been in Alex's casebook. Mitch had insisted that anyone she wanted to talk to come to the office since he didn't want Alex out of his sight. A line of frustration formed across his brow when he consid-

ered the missing pages from her casebook. He'd
scoured his backyard early that morning and hadn't
found anything. If it weren't for the fresh scratches on
her arm he'd still be inclined to believe she'd imagined
the whole thing. But the scratches were real. Just like
the fading bruises on her body. And the concussion that
had helped to steal her memory.

"Earth calling Sheriff Hayden," Roy taunted.

Mitch jerked to attention. He frowned. "Did I miss
something?"

"Only about the last ten minutes or so," Dixon
quipped, fighting a grin.

Annoyed, Mitch exhaled loudly and straightened in
his chair. He had to stop obsessing about Alex. "If it
was important, repeat it, if it wasn't, get the hell out
of here and find me a witness somewhere who saw or
heard something that'll give us a lead. There has to be
somebody."

Willis and Roy exchanged knowing grins. Dixon
glowered at first one and then the other.

His irritation mushrooming, Mitch threw up his
hands. "Am I missing something else?" He dared one
of them to say one wrong word.

"Nope, that's it." Dixon shoved to his feet. He
flashed a pointed look at his two junior deputies.
"We've got our orders, boys. Let's get moving."

Mitch gritted his teeth as the men filed out of his
office. If he thought for one second that Roy was stir-
ring up rumors, he would kick his butt. Jumping him
about it wouldn't be the best move, however. Roy
would just assume that his suspicions about Mitch and
Alex were right. And Mitch sure as hell didn't want
that.

Even if they were true.

"HEY, STELLA, you're looking good today."

Alex looked up, startled as well as annoyed, at Roy Becker. He'd stuck his head through the open doorway, effectively stalling her questioning of Stella Cramer. Not to mention the guy gave Alex the willies for some reason. There was something about his eyes. A needle of fear pricked her.

"Roy." Stella smiled and batted her ultralong lashes. "How are you this morning?"

"Just fine, Stel, just fine." He openly surveyed her long legs, expertly displayed by her miniskirt. "You planning on dropping by the club tonight?"

"You bet." She smoothed a hand over her miniscule halter-top. "My favorite band'll be there and it's Friday. A girl can't stay home on a Friday night."

Roy gave her a two-fingered salute. "See you then." He nodded to Alex, then disappeared. She shuddered inwardly, glad he was gone. Maybe it was that good old boy mentality that disturbed her. She glanced at Stella. Or, more likely, it was that macho attitude. Whatever it was, she didn't like the guy, not one little bit.

Stella didn't turn back to Alex until Roy was completely out of sight.

"The club?" Alex asked, curious about any hangouts Marija might have frequented.

"Yeah, the Down Under. You know music, dancing, drink." She waggled her eyebrows. "And lots of hunky guys."

"Did you ever see Marija Bukovak there?"

Stella considered the question for a couple seconds. "Yeah, once or twice." She shrugged. "Since all the cops and preppy guys from the college hang out there, most girls hit that place from time to time."

''Roy goes there?'' Alex wasn't sure what made her ask about Roy, but she had to know.

Stella grinned. ''All the time.''

After Stella had gone Alex studied her notes. She'd already checked in with Victoria. Anything to keep her thoughts away from Mitch Hayden. Even the echo of his name inside her head made her tremble. She was walking a tightrope here. She knew better. Though some of her memory might be misplaced, she knew better than to get involved with a player in a case. And Sheriff Hayden was definitely a player.

''Got a minute?''

The deep, sexy voice belonging to the subject of her reverie jerked her back to the here and now.

Alex produced a smile and struggled to ignore her body's instant awareness of his. ''Sure. What's up?'' She'd seen Mitch—there she went again calling him by his first name—meeting with the deputies working the homicide case. Somehow he always managed to work it where she wouldn't be around for their discussions. But he eventually filled her in—at least on the parts he wanted her to know.

Mitch sat down on the edge of Dixon's desk and settled that unnervingly intense gaze on hers. She didn't miss the slight softening. Could last night have affected him the way it did her? Probably not. But the mutual awareness was there.

''I'm sorry to have to tell you this, but Marija Bukovak's body has been found.''

Every ounce of emotion drained from her. She felt cold and numb. ''Where?''

''Just outside Nashville.'' Mitch looked away briefly before continuing. ''The M.O.'s Gill's. Talkington is pretty sure he did her.''

Fury detonated inside Alex, burning away the numbness, replacing it with outrage. ''I don't believe that.''

Mitch blew out an impatient breath. ''The evidence is pretty irrefutable. There was one thing about Gill's victims that wasn't released to the press.''

Alex grew still...her stomach suddenly feeling queasy. ''What's that?''

''He took a souvenir from each victim. A copycat wouldn't have known exactly what to take. It had to be Gill.''

Alex lunged to her feet. ''I want to see her. I want to go to the scene.'' She looked directly into Mitch's eyes. ''And then I want to talk to Gill again.''

Mitch stood, his fists clenched at his sides to hold back the mixed-up emotions twisting inside him. ''No way.''

''Then I'll speak to Talkington myself. I'm sure I can convince him to see reason.'' She hadn't missed the TBI agent's flirting. She felt certain she could persuade him.

Fury streaked through those sky-blue eyes. ''I'll place you under arrest and lock you in a cell first.''

''Zach will have me out within hours,'' she threatened.

Mitch shrugged, his gaze suddenly masked. ''Fine. But then you'll miss the meeting with Phillip and Nadine. I'm going over now to inform them of the news. If you'd had any questions, now would have been the time. But I guess that's out since I'm going to have to incarcerate you.''

He played dirty.

He knew how much she wanted that opportunity. Alex quickly regrouped her priorities. ''That won't be necessary, Sheriff,'' she said pointedly. ''As long as you agree to allow me an appointment with Talkington to discuss the autopsy and crime scene findings.''

One of those half smiles played with one corner of his mouth. "Done. Now, come on. We'll stop for lunch on the way.''

PHILLIP AND NADINE MALLOY lived in an ostentatious ranch-style country estate that alluded to their high standing in the community. They owned the land as far as the eye could see around their lovely home. When one arrived in the circular drive, a feeling of welcome was immediately experienced. But entering the stately home was an altogether different matter.

Cold yet elegant decor greeted visitors with a feeling of "don't touch.'' The housekeeper had shown Mitch and Alex to a pristine white—walls, carpet and furnishings—great room. The Malloys made their grand entrance a full five minutes later.

Phillip was a distinguished man in his mid-fifties. Alex could see a trace of resemblance between Mitch and Phillip, who was his uncle on his mother's side. Both men were handsome, tawny-haired and blue-eyed. Phillip proved even more charming than his nephew.

Nadine, however, was another story. She was cold and standoffish, clearly furious that Alex had been allowed to be a part of this meeting. The woman struck Alex as fiercely protective of her family. Her tight chignon and severely conservative attire made her look as untouchable as the interior of her home.

During the past thirty minutes, Mitch had, for Alex's benefit, walked Phillip and Nadine back through those last weeks with Marija, all the way to the day they took her to the airport. The Malloys presented a picture-perfect relationship and fond farewell.

But Alex didn't swallow it for a moment.

"They're certain the young woman they found is her then?" Nadine inquired, dabbing at her eyes with her husband's handkerchief.

Mitch nodded. "Her identity was verified by dental records, and her driver's license was found at the scene."

He'd failed to tell Alex the part about the driver's license. Why would Gill have left her ID lying around? According to Talkington's files he never had before. What else was Mitch leaving out?

"Does this wind up your investigation then, Ms. Preston?" Phillip Malloy asked.

Alex snapped to attention. She'd lost the thread of conversation. "I'm...not sure," she said slowly. Was that apprehension in the man's expression? Did he hope Alex would stop looking into Marija's disappearance now?

"We should be going," Mitch said, clearly anxious to separate Alex from his relatives. "I just wanted you to hear the news from me."

"Thank you, Mitch." Phillip shook his hand and slapped him on the back. "It was good of you to come by."

"There is one more thing," Alex interjected before Mitch could usher her from the room.

All eyes shifted to her. Mitch arrowed a warning in her direction. He'd said she could ask a question.

"Were either of you aware that Marija was pregnant?" she asked point-blank, going for the shock value.

Phillip Malloy steadied his wife who looked as if she might just faint. He looked to Mitch. "What is she saying?" he demanded, his face pale.

"Alex," Mitch said, his tone deadly, "this is not the time."

She glared back at him. She wasn't about to back off now. "Why not? I would think that Mr. Malloy would want to clear himself of any connection by submitting to DNA comparison testing."

The Malloys' collective gasps echoed in the room.

"Let's go." Mitch snagged her by the elbow and started toward the door. The look in his eyes was unforgiving. "We'll talk about this later."

"How could you bring her here like this?" Nadine shrieked. "She's trying to destroy our family!"

"Wait."

Phillip's soft plea stopped both Mitch and Alex in their tracks.

Mitch turned to his uncle. "I shouldn't have let this happen. I was wrong to let her come."

"No." Phillip shook his head. "I don't have anything to hide."

"Phillip!" Nadine commanded. "Don't say another word to this…this woman."

"What the hell's going on here?"

Alex swung around to find Roy Becker standing in the doorway. What was he doing here? What did he have to do with the Malloys?

"Somebody tell me what's happened?" Roy demanded.

Nadine stabbed a finger in Alex's direction. "She just accused your stepfather of getting that whore Marija pregnant."

Stepfather? Alex looked from Phillip to Roy, who wore a murderous expression.

"Get her out of here," Roy bellowed at Mitch. "I

don't want her hurting my family. Haven't you let her do enough damage already?'' he roared.

Roy was part of this family? Alex was stunned. How had she missed that? Or had she? Maybe she just didn't remember what she'd discovered about Roy.

"This is all her fault!'' Roy added. ''I should have let her die and then this wouldn't be happening.''

Let her die? Had Roy saved her life somehow?

Chapter Eight

Mitch had not spoken a word to Alex since they left the Malloy residence. He had banished her the moment they returned to his office. Deputy Willis stood guard outside Dixon's office where she was to do whatever she wanted, as long as she didn't leave the room. Willis had relayed that emphatic message with more official import than she'd seen the man display in the three days that she'd been hanging out at the sheriff's department.

She pushed her casebook aside, rested her chin in her hand and sighed. It bothered her that Mitch was so angry that he wouldn't even speak to her. That was a sure sign that he didn't trust himself to broach the subject without doing something he'd regret…like strangling her.

God, she was so confused. How had she allowed things to go so far south so fast? It wasn't bad enough that someone had messed up her head, she had to get involved with Mitch. She never allowed these kinds of mistakes.

Mitch and Roy were going at it in his office. Though she couldn't hear them with his door closed, she could see the emphatic gestures and angry expressions. There was no way to tell which one was the more furious. Both looked ready to battle to the death, and she hated that she was the reason.

Though she tried hard not to, her hungry gaze followed Mitch's every gesture, his every look. The moss-green, button-up shirt and faded jeans fit his body as if someone had designed the worn comfortable items especially for him. But the attire wasn't what had Alex mesmerized at the moment. It was the memory of that sculpted body. The smooth, tanned skin stretched over well-defined masculine muscle.

Mitch flared his hands in clear frustration at something Roy said, and Alex immediately recalled the way those skilled hands had touched her body. She shivered as warmth pooled inside her. The way he'd looked at her, touched and tasted her stole her breath even now. She couldn't explain it, couldn't even understand it, but somehow they connected on a level that transcended all else. There had definitely been something between them before she lost her memory, he just hadn't elaborated on it yet. And her brain apparently wasn't ready to go there.

She straightened and forced her gaze away from the man making her heart beat a little too fast. Alex stared at the casebook before her. Now that she'd had a chance to look it over more carefully, she realized that a great deal more was missing than she'd first thought. It was pretty much useless now, she'd gleaned about all she could from the few notes.

She looked over at her new notes from her conversation with Talkington. As usual Mitch had stood by his word. Talkington had called Alex to discuss Marija Bukovak about an hour after their arrival back at the office. Alex blinked back the moisture in her eyes. The body they'd found was that of Marija, Alex didn't doubt it. Not only did the dental records match, but she was wearing the silver necklace that matched her sister's. The scene indicated Gill's handiwork, but Alex still didn't buy it. Due to the extremely deteriorated condition of the body, the autopsy report would be a while in coming. Alex was surprised that Mitch had already told Talkington that the Bukovak girl might have been pregnant.

The man never ceased to amaze her. Her gaze went immediately to him. Whatever he'd just said to Roy, he wasn't happy about it. Roy stormed out of Mitch's office, slamming the door behind him. A chill of uneasiness slivered over her. Everyone in the reception area stopped and watched as he stamped away. Alex shifted her attention back to Mitch who was staring out the window behind his desk. For the first time in her entire career, she regretted having made a tactical maneuver. Had she not made that startling announcement—

Alex stopped midthought. What was she thinking? She shook off the confusing emotions muddling her thoughts. Her client might be dead, but Alex owed it to Jasna and Marija to find out what happened. To bring their murderer to justice. Not to mention she had to clear her own name. How could she regret a move in that direction?

She couldn't.

She drew in a deep, bolstering breath. She would not let Mitch Hayden, or her crazy infatuation with him, keep her from finding the truth.

Glancing at the clock on the wall, she decided it was time to check in with Victoria. Alex needed that anchor right now more than ever. She'd touch base with Ethan, too, and see if he had anything on the Malloys just yet. Work, that was the key to staying grounded. She had to remember that in this investigation she and Mitch were not on the same team. His loyalty lay with his family, hers with the Bukovak sisters. Time and hard work would reveal the winner.

Too bad there could only be one.

MITCH PICKED UP a shop cloth and wiped his hands. He stared through the darkness toward the house, or more specifically the kitchen window where he could see Alex putting away their dinner dishes. He threw the cloth onto the workbench and lowered the hood of his Jeep. There was nothing left to do but go inside. He'd put it off as long as he could.

He'd changed the oil in his Jeep and straightened up the garage. All in an effort to work off the fury he felt as much at himself as at Alex. But his efforts failed miserably. He still wanted to go in there and shake her. He hadn't said a word to her since leaving his uncle's house. Mitch had known that he wouldn't be able to control his emotions so he had avoided her all afternoon.

He switched off the garage light and started toward the house. He stalled after only a few steps and just stood there watching her graceful movements as she dried the pots and pans. Scenes from last night's love-making taunted him. Even now he could smell her skin, could taste her lips...and he wanted to do it all over again. He'd almost lost control when he sank into her that first time. He shook his head and averted his gaze from the woman playing havoc with his life.

Sex had never been like that before. Their bodies had meshed on a level that went soul deep. Alex had

touched him like no one else ever had. She'd lied to
him, tricked him into liking her, made him want to
protect her and then she'd struck where it would hurt
him most—his family. Family had always been extremely important to Mitch. The loss of his mother and
father had devastated both him and his brother. Phillip
and Nadine had been there when he needed them. Alex
threatened that precious link.

And still he couldn't turn off his feelings for her...or
his need to be with her. Somehow he would have to
avoid falling into last night's tender trap again. But
right now he had to go inside. He couldn't stay out
here all night.

Taking his time, he trudged the rest of the way to
the house, went inside and locked the door behind him.
Automatically he stopped at the hall table and listened
to his phone messages. Nothing important. Before he
could escape to the bathroom for a much-needed
shower, Alex appeared. Her arms were folded over her
chest in a protective but determined manner and her
eyes carried a haunted look.

"If you have a minute, I'd like to talk."

"We have nothing to discuss." Renewed anger
made his voice more gruff than he'd intended.

"Mitch," she implored, "don't do this. We have to
talk about what happened. It's going to take both of us
to solve this case. Acting childish isn't going to facilitate that end."

He glared at her. "Childish?" He shook his head
slowly from side to side. "I don't think you want to
hear what I have to say," he warned.

"Yell at me!" she demanded. "Do whatever you
need to do, but just don't shut me out like this."

Need clawed at him. Need to do just as she asked

and yell at her. Need to hold her. But he ignored it. "I don't have anything to say." He focused his gaze on the end of the hall and started in that direction.

"Wait." She snagged him by the arm and halted his determined exit. "Even if you don't have anything to say to me, I have something to say to you."

He told himself that he didn't want to hear anything she had to say, but he stood stock-still just the same. He couldn't force his feet to take the necessary steps away from her.

"I had to see Phillip's reaction to Marija's pregnancy. Giving him the news any other way would have lessened the impact. I had to know his first, true gut reaction."

Mitch glowered at the hand still resting on his arm, then at her. "And what was your analysis?"

She winced at his bitter tone. "Your uncle is hiding something. It may have nothing to do with Marija, but he's definitely hiding something relative to this case."

A new blast of fury hit Mitch. He snatched his arm away from her. "And just how the hell did you come to that conclusion? Because I damned sure didn't see it that way."

"You're too close. You can't be objective."

Mitch gritted his teeth and counted to ten.

It didn't help.

He braced his fists on his hips and glared down at her. Though she looked uneasy, she didn't retreat. "Why are you so determined to prove a connection between my uncle and Marija's disappearance?"

"I'm sorry this hurts you, Mitch, but—"

Holding his palms out stop sign fashion he silenced her. "Don't patronize me. Just tell me the truth. Let's put aside for a moment the fact that the TBI believes

Gill murdered the girl, and the fact that Phillip Malloy is a good, law-abiding citizen of this county, and you show me how you reached this conclusion."

She sucked in an unsteady breath. He watched the jerky rise and fall of her chest. He turned away. How the hell did she get to him so easy?

"I can't give you the answer you want. Whatever I knew is lost for the moment, along with most of my notes. But I know what I feel, and he's hiding something." She stepped around him to look directly into his eyes. "If he has nothing to hide, then submitting to a DNA comparison test shouldn't hurt anything but his pride."

Why did her words have to sound so reasonable? "I've heard all I want to on the subject," he said wearily. "Just drop it for now."

Mitch managed one step before she stopped him yet again. "Just tell me I'm right about that last part and I'll be happy."

He faced her, and admitted defeat when those big amber eyes reached out to him for some sort of reassurance. "I'll admit that if he has nothing to hide he shouldn't have a problem with the test. But—" he added when her expression lifted too much "—I can understand how betrayed they feel by me walking in there and allowing you to make that kind of allegation."

"I see your point there. They are your family," she conceded. "I should have warned you about what I had planned, but if I had, you wouldn't have allowed me to go."

"You're right," he admitted. "I wouldn't have."

"And then we would never have seen the horrified look on his face or the fear in his eyes."

Mitch exhaled noisily. He would not go quite that far. "It's done. I don't want to discuss it any further tonight."

"You didn't set this up," she offered. "I'll tell him that. It was me. It was all me."

Mitch closed his eyes and fought that same old battle. Part of him wanted to reach out to her and the other part, the saner, wiser part, wanted to turn away.

"Don't worry," she added anxiously. "I'll make him understand that you had nothing to do with it."

He laughed. "If that makes you feel bad, here's another news flash—Roy tried to resign this afternoon," Mitch ground out the words. "Said he didn't want to work for a man who would turn on his own family."

That really made her feel like pond scum. Mitch could see the remorse written all over her face. "Did you talk him out of it?" she asked in a small voice.

God, she knew just how to get to him.

Mitch shrugged. "For the time being."

She frowned suddenly. "What did Roy mean when he said he should have let me die?"

He'd wondered when she would get around to that. "I told you he'd stayed right by your side at the scene until the paramedics arrived."

She nodded, lines of confusion marring her smooth brow.

"According to Willis, you stopped breathing at one point and Roy resuscitated you."

Alex jerked with the flash of memory that accompanied Mitch's words. She couldn't breathe. She gasped. *Hey, man, what's wrong?* A mouth closed over hers and forced air into her hungry lungs.

Mitch was speaking to her. She could see his mouth moving, but she couldn't make out his words. Alex shook her head in an attempt to clear the other voices and images.

"Are you all right?" Mitch was shaking her now.

She pushed his hands away. "I'm okay." But she wasn't. Not really. Why had she stopped breathing? Her injuries hadn't been that severe. Or was it possible for the body just to shut down after a head trauma?

"We're not talking about this anymore tonight," Mitch snapped. "Neither one of us is up to it. Let's just give it a rest."

Alex nodded. "I had to know what he meant." The voice she'd remembered that had demanded to know what was wrong belonged to Willis. "Was Willis there with him the whole time?"

"Yeah. He and Roy were the first to the scene."

"Who called it in?" Alex didn't know why she bothered asking, or what it mattered, but she suddenly wanted to know.

Mitch shrugged those broad shoulders. "A group of teenagers who'd camped out that night. They stumbled onto the scene the next morning."

"Did you interview them?" Why hadn't he told her this before?

"Each and every one of them." His expression told her he wasn't pleased she'd felt it necessary to ask that question.

Ire lit inside Alex. "I'd like to interview them myself."

He sighed, impatient. "What's the point? They don't know anything."

That ire climbed in the direction of outrage. "You're shutting me out of this investigation," she accused. He was supposed to keep her fully informed. Obviously, he had as selective a memory as she unfortunately had at the moment.

"There's nothing to tell you," he said sharply. He glared at her with those icy blue eyes. "We don't have anything. No prints. No evidence, nothing. Except the stuff that points to you. Now, if you don't mind I'd like to hit the shower."

Before he could turn away, she asked, "What about the other?" She screwed up her courage. "The thing between you and me. You said that my dream was real. You're sure nothing was going on between us...before?"

"Not really." His expression was shuttered.

"What does that mean?" she demanded, stepping closer, forcing him to look at her.

"We had dinner, that's all."

She made a sound of disbelief. "I do recall a few of the moments we shared. It felt like a lot more than just dinner."

Something tried to peek through his mask of control, something she couldn't quite identify. "Did it?"

She blinked, uncertain if she should open herself up like this. He already knew too much about her. Had already touched her far too deeply. Instantly, she recognized what was peeking past his defenses—pain. "Yes, it did."

Had she hurt him somehow?

That iron mask of control slid firmly back into place. "Let's just say that we..." he lifted one shoulder in a less than enthusiastic shrug "...connected. But I was the only one who thought it was real," he added bitterly.

Confusion ruled her thoughts. "I don't understand. What are you saying?"

"You lied to me," he said tightly. "Told me you were just passing through on your way to Nashville. We talked for hours." His laugh was brittle. "And I believed every line you fed me. The next day I found out who you really were."

Why would she have purposely lied to him that way? To her knowledge, he had never been a suspect. Or had she just gotten caught up in that connection and hadn't wanted to ruin it by telling him the truth?

"Maybe I didn't want to tell you the truth because I didn't want that night to end," she suggested, giving voice to her thoughts.

He rolled his eyes. "Right. I was a fool once, Alex. I don't plan to make that mistake twice."

His words hurt more than she expected. "And what about last night?"

He looked directly at her then, anything he might feel carefully concealed. "Temporary insanity?"

"Thanks for clearing that up." She pivoted on her heel and stamped to her borrowed room. She didn't look back. Tears burned her eyes. She hated to cry. She slammed the door behind her and sagged against it.

Why did she care if last night meant anything to him? It was just sex. She closed her eyes and fought back the tears. Who was she fooling? Certainly not herself. Maybe it was payback for the way she had misled him that night she couldn't remember.

He knocked softly.

She tensed. She did not want him to know how much he'd hurt her.

"Look, I shouldn't have said that," he began tentatively, speaking through the closed door. "Last night was—"

"Sex," she snapped. "Go take your shower, Hayden, you're not the first man I've screwed and you won't be the last."

He didn't move for a long time. He just stood there, on the other side of the door making her want to open it and throw herself into his arms.

Finally, he walked away.

Alex swiped the moisture from her eyes and drew in a mighty breath. It was temporary insanity all right, and she had every intention of making sure it never happened again.

She had a case to solve. It was past time she got her head out of the clouds and focused on what she'd come here for. And it had nothing at all to do with Mitch Hayden. At least she didn't think it did.

Marija and Jasna were dead. Gill didn't kill Marija and Alex was certain Jasna had not committed suicide. That meant that someone who had the proper motivation had killed them both. The same someone who'd tried to kill Alex. She stepped away from the door, her conviction gaining momentum. The pregnancy had to be the key. The small amount of cocaine found in Miller's car sure didn't spell this kind of elaborate setup. It had to be the pregnancy. And Phillip Malloy had the most to lose—a wife and an election.

Now that was motivation.

Alex thought about Roy's reaction to his stepfather's dilemma. The guy was shaken pretty badly. With a temper that volatile, chances were he would break easily. Hell, he might even be the one. She shivered. All the evidence she remembered pointed to Phillip but she couldn't rule out Roy. Though he didn't live with Phillip and Nadine, Roy'd had access to the girl. She frowned. But would he kill one of his buddies? Alex had to know. She could get him to talk, she was sure of it.

A satisfied smile lifted her lips. Roy was the ticket. All she had to do was rattle his cage and she'd get some answers. But she needed him on neutral ground. *You planning on dropping by the club tonight? You bet.*

Stella was going to that club and so was Roy.

Alex grabbed one of the suitcases from near the closet and plopped it onto the bed. Thank goodness Mitch had brought all of her things here. She shuffled through her belongings until she came up with the one dress she'd brought with her. A very short, very tight, very black number that usually turned heads. She dug until she found the matching high heels. She grinned. And what was a little black dress without black undies. She grabbed the black thong panties and, on second thought, tossed back the bra.

She was going for sexy tonight. Roy was a flirt. She would use that to her advantage.

Alex surveyed her planned wardrobe. All she needed now was a ride. She grabbed her casebook from the dresser and flipped to the page where she'd written Stella's home number.

Repeating the number in her head so she wouldn't forget it, Alex opened the bedroom door and peeked into to the hall. The door to the bathroom was closed, but there was no sound coming from inside. She bit her lips and listened intently. The sound of footfalls made her jump back. Shoring up her courage she peeked around the edge of the door. Mitch went into the bathroom, clean jeans and a shirt hanging over his shoulder. He closed the door behind him.

Alex gathered her courage. As quietly as possible she tiptoed to the telephone on the hall table. Cringing, she picked up the receiver. The dial tone echoed down the silent hall. She stabbed the first digit of Stella's number to silence it. Going more slowly then so as not to make a mistake, she entered the rest of the number.

Just as Stella answered the call, she heard the water in the shower. Alex sagged with relief.

"Hey, Stella, this is Alex." She smiled at the bubbly woman's enthusiastic greeting. "Listen, Stel, I'm kind of in a hurry. Are you still planning to go to the club tonight?" The affirmative answer went on forever. "Good," Alex cut in. "Do you mind if I tag along with you?" Another enthusiastic response. "Great. Can you come get me right now? I'm at the sheriff's house, but I have to hurry if I'm going to go with you."

Stella assured Alex that she would be there in five minutes. Alex placed the receiver back in its cradle and hurried to her room. She made fast work of getting dressed, her discarded clothes landing where they would.

Listening carefully for any change in the sounds emanating from the bathroom, Alex walked barefoot to the front door. Once on the porch she slipped on her heels. Stella's car arrived within seconds, and Alex rushed down the steps and across the yard. She opened the door and climbed in with the perpetually happy waitress.

"Let's get out of here," Alex urged.

Stella winked. "Hey, girl, you ain't trying to give that good-looking sheriff the slip, are you?"

Alex grinned sheepishly. "That's exactly what I'm doing."

Stella squealed. "All right, girlfriend, let's do it." She stomped on the gas pedal and her car spun away from Mitch's house.

Yeah, Alex thought, *let's do it.*

MITCH TUGGED ON his shirt and gathered his discarded clothing and the towel he'd used. He stepped into the cool hall and shivered after acclimating to the steamy bathroom. He took his laundry to the washing machine and dumped it on top of the appliance. He'd worry about sorting later. Right now he had to talk to Alex. As much as he hated to give in, he just couldn't leave it this way.

He'd taken the time to dry his hair, but hadn't bothered to pull it back as he usually did. He tucked it behind his ears and went in search of the woman who was making his life a living hell.

It only took him about three minutes to determine that Alex was nowhere to be found. She had taken the time to change clothes, which meant she had some place special in mind and that foul play was unlikely. If someone had broken into the house to take her away, he doubted they'd want her to dress for the occasion. She hadn't taken any of her things other than what she was wearing. It was dark. His Jeep was still in the garage.

Someone had to have picked her up.

Mitch checked the caller ID unit. No one had called. He picked up the receiver and pushed redial. A distinctly feminine voice answered.

"Hello," Mitch began, uncertain what the hell he was going to say. "Is Alex there?"

"Uh-uh, honey, she and Stella are hanging at one of the clubs tonight. She didn't say which one, just that she was picking up a friend named Alex and going out. You sound cute, you need a date, honey? Looks like I've been stood up."

"No... Thanks." Mitch hung up. He swore. What the hell did Alex think she was doing going to a nightclub? He considered the clientele that frequented the places in this area and he had his answer.

She was looking for anyone who'd known Marija. But what she was going to find was trouble.

There was still someone out there who wanted her dead. And tonight, he might just find her.

Chapter Nine

Roy wasn't there.

Alex sat on a stool at the bar and tried not to give up hope just yet. She'd been here for almost an hour and Roy still hadn't shown.

The Down Under was a preppy place, Australian in decor as the name implied. Most of the clientele appeared to be under twenty-five, college students mostly. Alex concentrated hard on each area of the club. The bar, the dance floor and the clutches of small tables. None of it was familiar to her. If she'd come here before she had no recall of it and it wasn't mentioned in her notes...but then it could have been in the part that had been stolen.

She wondered briefly if Mitch ever came here. The ladies probably gravitated to him when he did. She pushed away that thought and the undeniable jealousy that accompanied it.

She cringed at the thought of what he might be doing at this very moment. Calling in the posse no doubt. He would not take this sitting down. But she couldn't worry about what he thought anymore. She had an investigation to conduct and she couldn't do it from under his thumb. As long as she was careful, watched out for herself, she'd be fine. It wasn't like this was the first time she'd carried on an investigation under dangerous circumstances.

Usually though, she had all her faculties in working order and had her weapon handy.

Alex dismissed thoughts of her amnesia and decided to work the room. She might as well see if anybody around here remembered Marija. She didn't have anything to lose and it would pass the time until Roy showed. If he showed.

She picked up her half-empty bottle of beer and slid off the stool. She surveyed the crowded place and selected a table with three young women drinking and eyeing the men who entered the club.

As Alex moved in that direction, she noticed Stella draped on a tall, good-looking guy several years her junior. Alex gave her the thumbs-up; Stella winked.

"Hey," Alex called out to the threesome seated around the table for four. "This seat taken?"

The three looked at each other, then at Alex and shook their heads in unison.

"Good." Alex settled into the chair and crossed her long legs in full view of any guy who happened by. She might as well attract as much attention as possible. The more bites she got, the more info she could glean.

During a brief lull in the loud music, the ladies introduced themselves and Alex did the same using an alias. Between the redhead, the blonde, the brunette, and their flashy, barely there, attire, Alex felt as if she'd slipped through the *Twilight Zone* and ended up on an episode of *Sex and the City*.

"A friend of mine used to hang out here," she added. "Marija Bukovak."

One girl nodded, the one named Tabitha. "Yeah, I

remember her. Didn't she like disappear or something?''

Alex adopted a sad expression. ''Yeah. No one knows what happened to her,'' she lied.

''I'll tell you what's strange,'' the redhead, Darlene, said. ''She was going with that deputy who got shot. Isn't that eerie?''

Pay dirt. Alex inclined her head in Darlene's direction. ''You mean Deputy Miller?''

Darlene nodded. ''I saw her here with him a couple of times right before she disappeared.''

''Me, too,'' the third girl, the brunette, Renae, added. ''They were pretty tight. You know, always whispering to each other and ignoring everyone else.''

Alex shrugged. ''Maybe they had a thing going,'' she suggested.

The three shared a look. ''Well, once she disappeared, Miller never came back here,'' Darlene said.

''It was weird,'' Tabitha put in. ''Those other guys, Arlon and Roy, they come here all the time. But Miller, he never came back, and he was big buddies with those two.''

Alex leaned closer into the circle. ''I heard that guy Miller was into the nose candy.''

All three shook their heads. ''No way. He was too uptight,'' Renae insisted.

''But now, Marija was a different story,'' Darlene interjected. ''She was a real cokehead.''

Alex resisted the urge to frown. ''Too bad.''

''Too bad for her,'' Tabitha said. ''But good for us. Whenever she was here, the guys always flocked to her. Well, at least until Miller started showing up with her.'' She flipped her long blond tresses over her shoulders. ''I don't see why either. She was too shy.''

"She wasn't that pretty," Renae said.

"But," Darlene cut in, "she had an accent. Guys love women with an accent."

All three giggled. Alex wanted to bang their heads together. Marija was dead and these three clueless nymphs were laughing at her. Of course, they didn't know she was dead. But Alex doubted it would change their attitude if they did.

Time to move on. Alex excused herself and headed back to the bar. She took another sip of her warm beer and considered what the girls had told her. So, Miller and Marija had something going. Sex and drugs? Was he supplying her with drugs in return for sex? At twenty-eight, he'd been a good deal older than Marija. Maybe that had been his game. A little of this for a little of that.

It grieved Alex to think that Marija had gotten involved with drugs. Her sister hadn't seemed to be aware of the problem. But then, they'd been apart for a good long while. With the kind of hardships they'd endured, it was easy to see how one or both could have turned to drugs for escape.

Alex was relatively certain that Mitch would go postal at the recommendation of testing Miller's DNA to see if he was the father of Marija's baby. He probably wouldn't like that idea any more than he did her request that Phillip be tested. And, Alex wasn't sure what it would accomplish. Even if Miller had something going with Marija, he couldn't have killed Saylor or Jasna. In Alex's book, that pretty much ruled him out.

Alex still couldn't believe she had missed the connection between Roy and the Malloys. He had to have known Marija fairly well himself. Maybe he should be tested, too. Outside a court order, Alex didn't see that happening. And it took evidence to sway a judge into issuing that kind of court order.

The warm beer flowed down her throat as she turned the bottle up once more. Alex plopped it down on the bar and surveyed the shimmying bodies on the dance floor. She hadn't been dancing in forever.

Mitch wasn't the only one with a social life that stunk. Alex had fallen way behind her peers in the dating game. That had proven one of the main draws between her and Zach. They were both extremely busy and working together as they did made things convenient, but that's it.

The image of Mitch Hayden formed in her head, stealing her breath and making her wish that things could be different. Even though she couldn't actually remember the night they had shared over dinner, she felt the bond that had developed. Last night's lovemaking, and that's what it had been, made her tingle each time she thought of the thorough way he'd touched her.

Alex was twenty-nine, she'd had several lovers over the years, but no one had made her feel the way Mitch did. Could it be somehow related to the bang on the head she'd suffered that made their lovemaking feel so…so intense? So earthshaking, so life altering? There had to be some explanation of why they were drawn together like two long lost missing halves of each other. But it was so the wrong time and place.

Ric Martinez had told her all about how he and Piper had fallen for each other. And a couple just couldn't get any more unlikely than those two.

Alex shook herself. What was she thinking? She and Mitch were merely two people thrown together during stressful circumstances. When the case was solved, the attraction would likely fade. They were on opposite sides of the game here. The adage opposites attract was likely at work.

The whole hoopla was probably nothing but chemistry and proximity.

Panning the club once more, Alex's gaze jerked back to the door. Roy Becker sauntered in.

"My, my, Roy, aren't you looking slick tonight?" Alex murmured. A shudder of something like revulsion quaked through her. Her lips drew down into a frown. What was it about him that rattled her so? Maybe she was confusing his presence at the scene with the other bad memories associated with that terrifying episode.

Roy shook hands and slapped high fives with his peers, and winked at the occasional attentive young lady as he crossed the room. He was decked out in clean jeans and shirt and his hair was spiked with gel. All in all, he looked pretty good for a good old boy that gave Alex the willies. And the ladies noticed him, including the clueless threesome she had spoken with earlier.

Roy scanned the room, his gaze jerking back to the bar, or more specifically to Alex. Fury tightened his features and he strode straight up to her.

"What the hell are you doing here?"

"I'm hanging out with my friend Stella," she retorted. "How about you?"

He glowered at her. "Are you checking up on me?"

She took another sip of her now flat beer, licked her lips and then smiled. "Don't be ridiculous, Roy. Why would I want to check up on you? It's your stepfather that interests me."

"Where the hell is Mitch?" he demanded, growing

antsy. He shifted his weight from foot to foot, obviously trying to decide what to do.

"He's probably looking for me."

"I'm calling Mitch right now," he threatened. His dark eyes glittered with uncertainty and maybe a little hint of something else.

"What's your hurry? Sit down, have a beer," Alex offered. She leaned forward, close enough to smell his cologne. She suppressed the urge to gag. "Tell me why I shouldn't believe your stepfather is involved in Marija's death."

Fury whipped across his lean face. His reply involved an explicit four-letter word and an implication to her.

"Come on, Roy," she urged, ignoring his building agitation. "You have to know more than you're telling. I sure would hate to have to get a court order for that DNA comparison testing."

Uncertainty crept back into his gaze. "My stepfather didn't touch that little whore."

Alex motioned for the bartender to bring them another cold one. She patted the stool next to her. "Sit, tell me why you didn't like Marija."

He looked startled at her suggestion. Alex held her breath, unsure if she'd pushed him too far. To her relief he straddled the stool next to her.

The bartender plopped two sweating bottles on the counter in front of them. The DJ had taken a break and the jukebox was playing, at a considerably lower volume than the DJ's raucous selections.

"Why did you call Marija a whore?" she asked, keeping her attention on the droplets of condensation sliding down the long-necked bottle. It took every ounce of courage and determination she possessed to keep up the front.

Roy drained half his beer, then wiped his mouth. "Because she was doing the horizontal mambo with Miller in exchange for drugs."

Alex pretended to be surprised. "Really? Do you think that's why Miller had drugs in his car the night he was killed?"

Roy shrugged. "How would I know?"

"Come on, Roy, help me out here. Was Miller getting the drugs for her from his connections on the street?"

"Maybe." He took another long pull from his bottle.

"Phillip and Nadine never suspected her drug problem?"

Roy glowered at her. "Leave my family out of this. They had nothing to do with what she was into."

"All right." Alex adopted a properly contrite expression. "I just have to be sure. You understand, don't you?"

His elbows propped on the bar, Roy rolled the long neck of the nearly empty bottle between his palms. "I know you're just doing your job. Mitch explained all that to me and my folks." Roy looked at her, long and hard. "But I don't have to like it."

"I'm sorry that my investigation is causing any upset for you and your family, but they were the closest people to Marija. Surely they suspected her drug use."

"She kept to herself. Nobody suspected anything. I only knew because of Miller."

He downed the rest of the beer. Alex gestured to the bartender for another.

"Ask Mitch," Roy said suddenly. "He knows she and Miller were doing the deed. I'm surprised he hasn't

already told you to take the heat off Phillip.'' Roy's
gaze connected with hers. ''Truth is, that's the only
reason I'm telling you now. I want you to leave my
family alone. I don't know who killed Miller, but if
you're looking for Marija's killer, he's already gotten
his. I'd bet money that Miller's the one who knocked
her up.''

''I appreciate your candor, Roy. That will be easy
enough to verify.''

Surprise flitted through his gaze again.

Another bull's eye. Alex took a tiny sip of her beer
to dampen her dry throat. The Miller scenario was all
just a little too pat. His story too closely resembled the
one she'd heard from the three young ladies just a little
while ago. But then again, maybe she just wasn't ready
to let Phillip Malloy off the hook so easily.

''I almost quit my job today,'' Roy told her, no
doubt vying for sympathy. ''Working in law enforcement is my life, but I was ready to give it up if the law
was going to allow decent folks to be harassed.''

Alex frowned as if she cared. ''I hope you've
changed your mind.''

He nodded, staring at the label on his beer bottle.
''Mitch talked me out of it.''

''I'm glad.'' She offered him the best smile she
could manage. ''I know how unhappy I'd be if I
couldn't do what I love.''

Roy grinned. ''It's hard to believe you're a P.I.'' He
gave her body a cool once-over. ''I mean, you should
be a model or something.''

''Why, thank you, Roy.'' She traced the mouth of
her bottle with her fingertip. ''I thought about that
once.''

Roy drained his second beer. ''I can see your pretty

face on the cover of magazines right now.'' He trailed a finger down her bare arm. She couldn't prevent a tiny shudder. ''How about a dance, Alex?''

She definitely did not want to dance with this guy. But she had him talking. She didn't want to lose his trust now. She smiled widely, as if she'd waited all night for this one request. The DJ rattled off something no one could understand then cranked a slow tune up so loud that Alex couldn't hear herself think.

She nodded in response to Roy's invitation and he led her onto the dance floor, not stopping until they were deep within the throng of dancers.

His arms went around her waist and he pulled her firmly against his lean body. Left with no choice, she draped her arms around his neck.

''You smell nice,'' he murmured in her ear.

Alex closed her eyes and ignored the roiling of her stomach. She didn't like being this close to him. As if reading her mind, he pulled her even closer.

''Thank you,'' she managed. Her attempts to put some space between them failed.

His right hand slid down over her hip and she tensed.

''Just relax, pretty lady, I'm gonna take real good care of you.''

The recall of a firm hand over her mouth and nose slammed into her brain like a bullet. Alex gasped.

''Hmm,'' Roy murmured. ''I like that, too.'' Both hands were on her buttocks now.

She struggled to control her body's reaction to the snatches of memory now bombarding her senses. She tried to breathe more slowly, more deeply, but it didn't work. *Is she breathing? I got it!* Roy's voice. That had been Roy's voice. The memory of his mouth closing over hers exploded inside her head next. Strong fingers closing around her throat, pulling her close. *Die, bitch,* reverberated in her ears. She couldn't place that whispered voice.

Alex struggled against Roy's hold. Déjà vu swamped her yet again, making her feel as if she'd been in this position before. "Roy, I—"

"Just relax." He tightened his arms around her. "You're safe with me."

Alex trembled in spite of her best efforts.

He chuckled softly in her ear. "You don't have to be afraid of me, Alex. I'm a deputy. I'm sworn to uphold the law."

She sucked in a deep breath and tried desperately to regain her composure. The memories had disoriented her. She wanted to be anywhere but here at the moment.

"Still don't have your memory back, huh?" he asked, his breath fanning her cheek.

She shook her head, certain her voice would be too unsteady if she tried to respond verbally.

"You should try that hypnosis Peg recommended. It works all the time in the movies."

Hypnosis? "What hypnosis?" she croaked.

"Peg said some doctor hypnotized her husband and he quit smoking." Roy nuzzled her neck. "She thinks he could help you get your memory back."

"I'll have to talk to Peg about that," she said for lack of anything else to say. She shuddered again at the feel of his lips on her shoulder. She tried to push him away.

"We should go somewhere more private," he suggested. "It's too loud here." He kissed her ear. "I could show you a hell of a good time, pretty lady."

She had to get away from him. She felt sick to her stomach. Her head was spinning.

He pressed her hips against his, showing the evidence of his desire for her. "Come on, Alex, it'll be fun," he murmured.

The music stopped. "I have to go to the ladies' room." She struggled out of his hold and plowed through the crowd of dancers without looking back.

Her heart hammered so hard she was sure it might jump out of her chest. She clamped her hand over her mouth when the urge to heave threatened to overwhelm her. She needed water. She needed air. Her head was spinning. She staggered toward the sign that read Rest rooms. She'd made a mistake coming here. Maybe Stella would take her back to Mitch's place.

Another wave of memories slammed into her. A gloved hand closed over hers and forced her to pull the trigger on her weapon. Alex jerked to a stop halfway across the crowded club. The faces, the sounds faded. The blast of the weapon sounded in her ears, she felt the recoil reverberate through her body. Miller was dead, slumped in the car seat behind the steering wheel. Fire blazed from the weapon trained on her face. The sound of a horn blowing, of loud rap music thumping and then nothing.

Time and place slowly came back into focus. The dance tune jumping from the DJ's massive speakers. The limber bodies gyrating to the sound. Scantily clad waitresses weaving between tables, delivering drinks. The strobe of colored lights flashing around the room and across the ceiling.

"Oh, God." Alex fought a surge of nausea and stumbled the remaining steps to the hallway where the rest rooms were. Staying vertical proved extremely difficult. She needed desperately to throw up, and even more critically to allow the darkness threatening her consciousness to come, bringing blessed relief.

Her vision dimmed with the next bout of dizziness. She groped the wall to find her way. The bitter taste of bile rose in her throat.

She groaned, whether out loud or mentally, she couldn't say. She had to get to that bathroom and splash some water on her face.

Strong fingers clamped like a vise on her arm and swung her around. Her body tried to crumple but she fought the urge. It took her a moment to determine whether it was real or just another vivid memory. She struggled against the hold that was all too real.

"What the hell do you think you're doing?"

It was Mitch. Thank God. She tried to focus on his face, but her eyes wouldn't quite do the job.

He shook her. "Answer me, dammit."

She sucked in a breath. "I...I think I need some air."

She wilted. Mitch scooped her up into his arms and strode toward the rear entrance.

Chapter Ten

"Better now?" Mitch regarded the woman leaning against his Jeep with a mixture of fury and worry. She'd looked ready to pass out when he found her.

Alex nodded and drew in a long, deep breath. "I just needed some air."

Mitch wanted to rail at her, but at the same time he needed to make sure she was okay. "You're sure you don't need to see a doctor?" The memory of the seizure she'd suffered that day at the clearing was still painfully vivid in his mind. She hadn't been gone long enough to get the kind of alcohol buzz that would make her this shaky.

She shoved a handful of hair behind her ear and slowly lifted her gaze to his. "I suppose you're upset that I took off on you like that."

"Upset is something you feel when your favorite football team loses a game they should have won. This is not upset." He gritted his teeth to hold back the proof of his words.

She straightened away from the vehicle and smoothed a hand over her form-fitting dress. "I had to talk to some of Marija's friends and find out what they knew about who she'd been seeing at the time of her disappearance. Just because she's dead doesn't mean this is over for me.''

Unable to stop himself, he allowed his gaze to travel the length of her, from all that dark hair, over that slender body, down those long legs, and to her high-heeled shoes. Moonlight washed over her, enhancing her beauty with a silvery glow. He retraced his path, going a little slower this time. The dress fit like a glove, hugging her slender curves in a way that made his mouth parch. The outline of her unrestrained breasts only made bad matters worse. And the silky black material served as a gut-wrenching contrast to her creamy skin.

Mitch jerked his attention back to the problem at hand. ''Do you know how crazy it is for you to sneak out like this? We still can't be certain that someone isn't watching for the opportunity to take you out.''

''I had to,'' she argued. ''You would never have allowed me to come. And I sure wasn't going to get anyone talking with you hanging around.'' She tapped the star he wore. ''That little accessory has that effect on people you know. They fear reprisal so they keep their mouths shut.''

Mitch shook his head. ''I think that knock on the head affected your ability to think straight.''

Alex opened her mouth, no doubt to refute his assessment, when a car skidded to a stop a few feet away.

Mitch went on instant alert. He didn't recognize the blue sedan. The driver's side window powered down.

''Hey, girl, I see that good-looking sheriff found you.''

Stella from the diner. Mitch relaxed.

''He found me all right,'' Alex grumbled.

"I was looking for you inside. I thought maybe you might want to go over to the Hideout with me."

Mitch shot Alex a glower. No way was she going to that sleazy place.

"I guess not, but thanks anyway."

Stella winked. "Don't sweat it, girlfriend. I got Lorraine here to go with me." She hooked a thumb in the direction of her passenger. "See ya around!"

Stella spun out of the parking lot in a spray of gravel. Mitch hoped like hell she hadn't been drinking. Maybe on the way home he'd drive by the Hideout and make sure her car was safely in the lot.

Alex watched Stella go and wished she was going with her. She stole a glance at Mitch and cringed inwardly. Though he was doing an exemplary job holding back his fury, she could see that he was seriously angry. She supposed that her bout with the flashbacks was all that had saved her from the full measure of his wrath. Right now she just wanted it over. Two clashes with him in one day were more than enough. Why drag it out?

"What are you going to do? Lock me up now?"

Mitch turned that fiery gaze back on her. "That's exactly what I ought to do."

She crossed her arms over her chest and glared right back at him in defiance. "Fine. If that's your intent, why don't we get it over with rather than beating around the bush? I don't suppose you're going to take in to consideration that I didn't come alone and I was careful."

He surveyed the dark parking lot, then glared at her. "Get in."

Apparently he wasn't going to give her any consideration whatsoever. She lifted her chin another notch.

"I don't think so. Whatever you have to say, you can say it now, then I'll decide if I'm getting in or not."

"I said get in," he repeated, a dangerous quality in his tone.

Her courage wavered, but she held her ground. "No."

He flung his arms skyward and swore hotly, then he pinned her with a gaze that was nothing short of scorching. "First you claim someone is trying to kill you, then you flit around here like you don't have a care in the world. Don't you know the risk you took coming here or did you forget?"

Alex met that fierce gaze head-on. "I had a lead to follow up on."

"What kind of lead?" he demanded.

No way was she telling him that she came here to find Roy. Instead, she turned the tables on him. "Why didn't you tell me there was something going on between Marija and Deputy Miller?"

He looked taken aback. "Where'd you come up with an idea like that? As far as I know Miller never met the girl."

She wanted to tell him that Roy said differently, but that would never do. If Roy got wind that she'd told Mitch what he said, he might not tell her anything else. And she definitely had more questions for him.

"Some of the girls inside told me," she said, which was true.

Mitch shook his head. "If there was anything going on between the two, Miller never mentioned it."

"Why would he?" Alex scoffed. "Especially if he'd gotten her pregnant and then killed her."

Renewed fury tightened Mitch's features. "Miller didn't kill anybody."

"If you're so sure about that, then you won't have a problem comparing DNA when the autopsy comes back verifying Marija's pregnancy." Alex held her breath as she waited for his reply.

Just when she'd decided he wasn't even going to bother answering her, he said, "That sounds reasonable. I'll tell Talkington to arrange it as soon as possible."

Alex was the one taken aback this time. He'd said yes. God, it was almost too easy.

"But first," he qualified, "you have to tell me why you really came here."

Uh-oh. He hadn't bought her excuse. Though it had been partially true.

"I told you why I came," she evaded.

He shook his head. "Try again."

Alex backed against the Jeep, away from that penetrating gaze. "I guess I'm ready to go now."

He moved in on her, trapping her between the vehicle and his powerful body. "Why did you hitch a ride with Stella and come here tonight?"

Alex moistened her lips and tried to come up with an acceptable excuse, but there was none.

He propped one arm on top of the vehicle and leaned even nearer. His freshly showered scent folded around her, made her ache for his touch. All that golden hair fell forward, momentarily capturing her complete attention.

"There had to be a reason or you wouldn't have taken the risk," he insisted.

Her nerves jangling and her body overreacting to his, she blurted, "I came to see Roy."

Oh, damn.

The moon provided just enough illumination for her

to get a good look at his furious expression. Alex drew back but the edge of the seat stopped her.

The muscle in his tightly clenched jaw flexed. "Do you have any idea how angry Roy was at you this afternoon? Showing up at his favorite haunt when he's had a few beers was not a smart move. He could have…" Mitch fell silent, clearly grappling for control.

"Are you saying that Roy gets violent when he's had a few?"

Those icy blue eyes flickered with rocketing irritation. "I'm saying," he ground out the words, "that you could have been on the receiving end of a heated outburst."

A theory formed in Alex's mind. "Do you think he would go ballistic if some girl he considered unworthy of him told Roy he'd gotten her pregnant?"

Mitch slammed his fist against the Jeep. "You never give up, do you? First it's Phillip, then it's Miller, now it's Roy."

Alex inclined her head in agreement. "I'd say that pretty much pins down the right suspects."

"Get in the damn Jeep."

His last sliver of patience had vanished. Mitch just wanted to get her out of here. He didn't know what the hell he was going to do with her, but he didn't want her on the streets. Her nosing around was going to get her into serious trouble. He supposed Roy was as much a suspect as anyone else, but Mitch didn't have to like it.

"I said get in," he snapped when she didn't move.

She fixed him with a look that spelled trouble. "Roy asked me to go some place more private with him. He seemed more than happy to talk to me. Maybe I should take him up on his offer."

Something thick and dark engulfed Mitch. Something that felt far too much like raging jealousy.

"In fact, I think he kind of likes me in spite of—"

Mitch silenced her with his mouth.

He didn't want to hear any more of her excuses. He didn't want to talk anymore about the case.

His kiss was hard and punishing, just like he meant it to be. His heart hammered in his chest like a sledgehammer. She tried to push him away at first, but then her fingers fisted in his shirt and pulled him closer. She trembled, then melted against him. The thought crossed his mind that he shouldn't do this...but he opted not to think for now.

He wanted to feel.

He wanted Alex. Again.

He smoothed his palms over her satiny thighs and beneath the hem of that short black dress that made him too crazy to reason or even to think. The swell of her firm buttocks filled his hands and his body jerked with reaction. Instantly, he hardened like a rock. He deepened the kiss, thrusting his tongue inside her mouth as his fingers found and traced the thong of her panties. She whimpered and he stroked that sensitive path again.

Her hand slid between their bodies. She stroked the stiff bulge of his erection through the denim of his jeans. He groaned, needing desperately to feel the soft warmth of her palm against him, and wanting even more to be inside her pumping hard toward the release steadily building inside him.

He broke the kiss long enough to murmur, "Get in. We can't do this here."

His hands on her waist, he lifted her into the Jeep

and she scooted over to the passenger's side. Mitch climbed in and started the engine.

"Hurry," she breathed, her plea urgent, her fingers fisting in his shirtsleeve. "You started this, don't make me wait."

He shoved the Jeep into gear and roared out of the parking lot. He pushed the limits of the speed zones as he sped across town in record time. He could feel her watching him, but he didn't dare look at her for fear of not making it the rest of the way home. Speaking was too risky as well. One wrong word and the spell would be broken. As much as he knew he should, he didn't want that.

He swore when the last traffic signal before leaving Shady Grove proper behind turned red, forcing him to stop. His fingers tightened on the wheel, his palms sweating with the need pounding in his loins. He wanted to touch her. He was already breathing hard, his whole body primed for mating with hers.

She leaned over and kissed him, her lips trailing along his jaw until she found his mouth. Instinctively his fingers threaded into her hair, holding her more firmly against him. One long leg slid over his lap until she straddled him, her back to the steering wheel. The light was probably green now but he didn't care, he couldn't take his mouth from hers. Her tongue tangled with his at the same time that she pressed down against him, the heat between her thighs burning him through the worn cotton.

A horn blared behind them. Difficult as it proved, Mitch dragged his mouth from hers and concentrated on moving forward. Her fingers buried in his hair, Alex traced the cleft of his ear with her tantalizing tongue. Mitch resisted the urge to close his eyes in ecstasy. He had to focus on the road before them, but she wasn't making it easy.

Her hips undulated against his lap, her mouth doing something equally wicked to his throat. His erection pulsed, hard and too close to the edge for comfort. He needed to be inside her. With one hand on the wheel, he cupped her thigh, then explored that sensitive flesh until he found the hot, wet spot he'd been looking for. She cried out when his finger parted her feminine folds. Her movements became more frantic as that same finger eased inside her. She ground her pelvis against him, taking him deeper. A second finger slipped inside and her inner muscles spasmed around him. Her teeth sank into his neck. He groaned savagely.

Mitch barely made the left turn onto his road. She was riding him hard and fast now. Her breathing as ragged as hell, her slick walls clenching around his fingers. He skidded to a stop in front of his house at the same instant that she came. Her scream of release sent his blood searing through his veins and his pulse pounding in his ears.

He snatched his keys from the ignition and stumbled out of the Jeep with her clinging to him, her body still throbbing with release. He maneuvered the front steps; stumbled across the porch. Her mouth sealed over his as he attempted to slide the key into the lock. It took three tries, but he was so lost to their desperate kisses that he barely noticed.

After kicking the door shut and flipping the dead bolt he tossed his keys in the general direction of the hall table and bumped into the nearest wall. Alex ripped his shirt open, sending buttons pinging to the hardwood floor. She shoved the shirt off his shoulders and kissed the center of his chest. Her sweet mouth closed over one nipple and he roared with savage need. There was no time for any more foreplay, he had to be inside her.

Mitch dragged her panties off, then wrenched his jeans open, freeing himself. He hiked her dress above her hips and coiled her legs around his waist. He swore at the awkward position and hitched her bottom a little higher. His tip nudged her dampness. She moaned with pleasure. Pressing her back against the wall, he plunged deep inside her, stretching her tight feminine walls until she cried out. When he would have pulled back, she clutched his shoulders and urged him on with unintelligible words. Her feet, high heels and all, locked at the small of his back, she arched her hips, meeting each of his thrusts, sinking him deeper inside her.

One more thrust and he exploded with release. As his movements slowed, her tight, clenching muscles milking the last remnants of climax from him, the only sound was their frantic panting. He kissed her soft shoulder and cursed himself for being too brutal. He'd been so ready by the time they got through the door it was a miracle he hadn't come the moment he entered her.

Their surroundings slowly drifted into consciousness. The house was silent and dark. It was late. He anchored her to him, one arm locked around her waist, the other supporting her lush bottom. He walked, their bodies still intimately joined, to his bedroom and lowered her to his bed.

Alex shivered at the feel of the cool sheets beneath her. The bare skin of his chest was damp with sweat. He kissed her forehead, her nose, her hungry mouth and then down the column of her throat. She felt him hardening inside her all over again and she smiled, her heart still pounding so hard she could hardly catch her breath.

He nibbled then sucked her jutting nipples through the silk of her dress. She arched her back in approval. His arousal thickened, filling her, stretching her all over again.

And then he moved.

The movements were slower, but deeper, the thickness of him dragging along her tingling feminine flesh causing a sensuous friction that had her fever mounting all over again. The muscles that moments ago had been sated and relaxed now tensed in anticipation of her new building climax. She locked her legs around his and met each hammering thrust until an even more powerful release shuddered through them simultaneously. They collapsed together, their harsh breathing breaking the quiet of the dark room.

Long minutes later when the sweat had dried and breathing had returned to normal, Mitch still held her close to his chest. She could feel his heart beating steadily.

"Don't ever do that again," he whispered, his voice raw and filled with emotions she couldn't quite sort.

She smiled against his bare skin. "What? Have wild, hot sex with you?"

A possessive hand glided along her spine and pressed her intimately against him. "You know what I mean."

She sighed and trailed a finger around one perfect pec. "I promise I won't do it again unless I have to."

He swore softly. "At least give me the chance to go with you."

Alex drew back and looked up at him, trying desperately to see his eyes in the sparse moonlight filtering in through the windows. "All right."

She refused to analyze what that request meant. If she put too much stock in it, she would only wind up with a broken heart. She closed her eyes and winced inwardly. God, it was too late. Her heart was involved. She tamped down the emotions that stirred with the thought. Whatever she thought she felt, one thing was certain, Mitch wouldn't be experiencing the same thing. This was likely just another male-female encounter as far as he was concerned.

"Another thing," he said, his voice still husky from a double climax. "That wasn't just sex."

THIS ISN'T the first time he's gotten a young girl pregnant.

Alex tried to claw her way from the nightmare invading her dream of making love with Mitch. She didn't want to hear this. She wanted to feel languid and safe. The way she did in Mitch's arms with him filling her body and soul.

About fifteen years ago he did the same thing. He covered it up that time by paying the girl off. This time he may have done something much worse.

Alex groaned. She didn't want to know. Go away, she told the unwanted voice. *Just go away.*

I can't go away, Alex. You promised to help me. Don't let him get away with what he did to my sister. He can't escape his past. All you have to do is dig deep enough.

Alex shook her head. Mitch. She wanted to dream about Mitch.

He was furious. Lines of rage were etched in his handsome face. Alex hated herself for what she had done. She'd felt something with him…and now it was for nothing. Stay away from my family, he commanded. Stay away from me. And if you don't stop nosing around in my county, you'll be sorry.

Alex jerked awake. She sat straight up. She couldn't breathe. Mitch stirred beside her. The purple and gold hues of dawn were streaking across the room. She stumbled from his bed, almost falling in her haste. He'd threatened her. He knew something about Phillip's past. Something that had a major bearing on Marija's disappearance.

I was told he's done this before.

Jasna's voice. She'd told Alex about another time, fifteen years ago, when Phillip had gotten another young girl in trouble. Having heard rumor of that long hidden fact had been the deciding factor in Jasna's mind that Phillip was somehow responsible for her sister's disappearance.

Alex shoved her tousled hair back from her face and snatched up the closest item she could find to cover herself. Mitch's scent enveloped her as did his shirt. She trembled and fought the urge to cry. He'd threatened to make her sorry if she didn't leave his family alone and stop digging around in his county. He was protecting his uncle. How far would he be willing to go to cover for him?

A shudder wracked her trembling body. She had to get out of here.

"Alex, what's wrong?"

She froze, unable to even take a breath.

He climbed out of bed, gloriously naked, his full-grown morning arousal making her heart beat even faster. She squeezed her eyes shut and blocked his image. She couldn't trust him. How had she missed that?

Blood is thicker than water.

"Hey." His fingers curled around her upper arms. "Did you have another nightmare? God, you're shaking."

She forced her eyes open and looked directly into his. "Take your hands off me."

His expression lined with concern. "Just tell me what's wrong." He looked so worried. How could he do that?

She twisted out of his hold. "Don't touch me again." She sucked in a shaky, but much-needed breath. "You're covering for Phillip."

He sighed and plowed his fingers through his hair. "Not that again."

"You threatened me," she snapped. "You told me I'd be sorry. Did you think I wouldn't remember until it was too late?"

He looked directly at her then and Alex saw the truth of her words in his eyes.

Chapter Eleven

Alex waited, her impatience growing with each passing minute, for Ethan to return her call. He'd left a message with Peg after Alex and Mitch left the office yesterday to go to the Malloy house. She hoped he'd found something on Phillip. Specifically she needed proof that what Jasna had told her was true. Alex had no recall of looking into Jasna's allegation. But she must have. She would never have put off checking out that kind of lead.

And that would explain a lot. It would certainly justify her gut feeling that Phillip was hiding something. Not to mention it would lend credibility to why she'd chosen to avoid telling Mitch the truth that first night. She'd obviously known his connection to Phillip. But that connection hadn't stopped her from falling for the guy.

She blew out a frustrated breath and stared at the pages scattered on the desk before her. The last thing she needed to think about was her foolish feelings for Mitch. She'd really screwed up this time. Not only had she gotten involved with a player in a case, she couldn't trust him.

He'd threatened her when she was guilty of nothing but following the leads in her investigation.

He was a cop. He should understand that better than anyone.

Mitch had tried repeatedly last night and this morning to explain that he'd only been angry and blowing off steam, but Alex just couldn't trust her instincts where he was concerned. Though her heart told her he was telling the truth and that he cared for her…*blood is thicker than water*.

Why had that phrase stuck in her head?

Mitch stepped out of his office, drawing her attention as easily as if her very survival depended upon seeing him. He propped one hip on the edge of Peg's desk and reviewed the messages she'd taken for him.

As usual, his hair was restrained at his neck. But it hadn't been last night. Last night the tawny mane had fallen around his shoulders. She'd tangled her fingers in the silkiness of it. She'd traced that square jaw with her tongue, kissed him until she couldn't breathe. Her heart skipped a foolish beat. The way he'd held her in his arms after their lovemaking…so tenderly, as if he had deep feelings for her.

She shook off that line of thinking. None of it was real. She was confused. The head injury most likely was the cause. She'd never had this kind of problem maintaining her objectivity before.

Mitch looked straight at her. Her breath caught.

The telephone extension on Dixon's desk rang, jerking Alex from the trance she'd immediately slipped into when faced with that mesmerizing gaze. She turned away from those hypnotic blue eyes and snatched up the receiver.

It was Ethan.

"I think I have what you're looking for, Al."

She massaged the ache that had started in her forehead. "Great. I could use a good lead about now." Who was she kidding? She could have used a good lead days ago. Then maybe she could have saved Jasna's life. Alex closed her eyes against that painful reality. Both Jasna and her sister were dead, nothing she could do now would change that. But she owed it to them to bring their murderer to justice.

"Well, you were right, Phillip Malloy is hiding a dirty little secret."

Alex held her breath, hoping it would fit with what she'd remembered from one of her conversations with Jasna.

"Fifteen years ago when he was Professor of Law at Ole Miss, he got involved with one of his students, Kari Brown."

I was told he's done this before.

A chill sank all the way to Alex's bones.

"When his pupil discovered she was pregnant, he insisted she get rid of the problem or else."

"Or else," Alex echoed. "What was the or else?" Why couldn't she remember any of the conversation with the Brown woman? Alex had to have been the one to locate her.

"She didn't take a chance on finding out. She took the money and disappeared. She never spoke of it again until you found her."

So the dream was right. Jasna heard the rumor and, with Marija missing, feared the worst for her sister. She'd hired Alex to find out if the rumor was true and to try and find Marija. Alex had found the woman. Her brow furrowed into a frown. Not even a glimmer of memory came to mind.

"Kari won't testify against him. She's no longer afraid of Malloy, but she doesn't want her husband or the kid to know it happened. I don't know how much weight the information carries if we can't use it to bring him down."

Alex's gaze riveted to the reception area. Mitch was striding in her direction.

"Trust me, Ethan, this is just what I needed. Look, I'll call you back." She hung up without waiting for his goodbye.

Mitch paused in the doorway of Dixon's office. The grim line of his mouth and the solemn look in his eyes told her that whatever he had to say, it wasn't good.

"What's happened?" Alex stood, needing to feel more in control.

"Stella's dead."

Alex grasped the edge of the desk to stay vertical.

"How?" she managed to choke out.

Mitch scrubbed at his forehead with the heel of his hand. The same exact spot where pain pounded between her eyes as well. He let go a weary breath then locked his gaze back on hers.

"Her car ran off the road at Buncombe Crossing. I have to go up there. They're recovering the vehicle now."

Alex rounded the desk. "I'm going with you."

He looked ready to protest, but changed his mind when faced with the determination in her eyes. "All right," he acquiesced.

When she would have brushed past him to go out the door, he blocked her path. "Tell me what it'll take to make you believe what's happening between us is real."

Alex didn't look at him. If she did, she'd give in and

she just wasn't ready to take that risk again so soon. "We'll talk about that when this case is solved."

He lowered his arm and Alex moved past him.

When this case was over she'd be going back to Chicago. Whatever was or wasn't between them would only be a bittersweet memory then. Her heart squeezed at the thought, but she ignored it. She had to.

THE AMBULANCE was just leaving when Alex and Mitch arrived on the scene. A couple of tow trucks, the police and a reporter from the local paper were milling around the narrow shoulder of the road and looking down thirty feet into a deep, wooded ravine.

The officer directing traffic had kept the curious bystanders to a minimum, but a few lingered fifty or so feet away.

"How's it going, Hayden?" A Tennessee state trooper stopped making notes long enough to shake Mitch's hand.

"What have you got so far?"

Alex studied the straining tow truck that was attempting to drag the car from its deep grave. The winch's occasional grind and groan of protest punctuated the slow retrieval.

"The guys who removed the bodies from the wreckage spotted a few beer bottles, considering last night was Friday night, it's likely the two ladies were drinking. We won't know for sure for a day or so."

"Two ladies?" Alex asked.

He nodded. "A Lorraine Bradford was a passenger in the vehicle."

I got Lorraine here to go with me. Stella's wicked grin flashed in Alex's mind. She felt sick to her stomach.

The winch squealed with the tension of lifting the car the last few feet. The trooper, Mitch and Alex moved instinctively in that direction.

Alex walked around the tow truck to the vehicle once it was pulled up onto the road. She peeked in the open window and noted the empty beer bottles the medics had spotted. Blood was splattered on the dash, the windshield and the upholstery of the front seat. The damage to the windshield indicated that neither of the occupants had been wearing a seat belt.

Alex closed her eyes and shook her head slowly from side to side. The memory of the vibrant waitress haunted her.

"That would be my guess."

The trooper's comment dragged Alex from her disturbing thoughts. He and Mitch were studying the rear end of the blue sedan. Alex slowly made her way to where they stood.

The trooper squatted near the bashed-in trunk. "Looks like the other vehicle might have been black. An SUV or pickup truck judging by the impact points."

Mitch turned to Alex. "It looks like someone rammed into Stella several times, forcing her off the road."

Alex stared at the car she'd ridden in just last night. "Everybody liked Stella. Why would anyone want to do that?"

She didn't realize she'd spoken out loud until Mitch responded.

"Who knew that you were at the club with Stella last night?"

Alex looked from Mitch to Stella's car. She was supposed to have been in that car with Stella. Would have been if Mitch hadn't dragged her away from the club. Without answering Mitch's question, Alex wandered back to the driver's side of the car. The image of Stella sitting behind that wheel and laughing enthusiastically evolved before her eyes.

Stella was dead.

And it was Alex's fault.

"Yo, Sheriff, Peg's trying to reach you."

Alex glanced back to where Mitch stood. Roy and Willis had just gotten out of their Raleigh County Sheriff's Department cruiser and were headed in his direction.

"Too bad about Stella and—"

Roy stopped midsentence when Alex stepped into his line of sight. He looked startled, but quickly recovered. "Ms. Preston," he acknowledged with a dip of his head.

"Yeah," Willis continued where Roy left off before spotting Alex. "She was the best waitress the diner had."

Roy flicked an uneasy glance in Alex's direction then turned his attention back to Mitch. "Don't forget to call Peg," he reminded. "Come on, Willis, we gotta get going."

Alex watched the two drive away. Every instinct warned her that Roy knew a great deal more than he'd told her last night. Seeing her after he'd let a few things slip last night must have shaken him. One way or another Alex had to find a way to get some more one-on-one time with him. Phillip Malloy was savvy at keeping secrets, he was a politician after all, and he'd had fifteen years of experience. But Roy, he was a different story. He was the key to solving this mystery, Alex was sure of it.

"I APPRECIATE IT. Will do." Mitch hung up, ending the call he'd made to the medical examiner's office. He wanted the preliminary autopsy report as soon as possible. Stella's car would be gone over by the techs to try and determine the make of the automobile that had forced her off the road. The paint would identify the automobile manufacturer. They already knew the vehicle was either an SUV or a truck, something with a high profile and black in color.

Mitch's attention shifted to Alex. She sat in front of his desk studying the trooper's accident report and the identification of the victims.

She looked up, her gaze seeking out his. "Lorraine had long dark hair."

Mitch nodded. "I know." Lorraine had been Stella's roommate, the woman he'd spoken to last night. She'd obviously decided to catch up with her friend when her date didn't show.

Alex lowered her gaze to the report once more. "Whoever did this thought I was in the car with Stella." She looked at Mitch. "If I hadn't called her—"

"Don't do this." He rounded his desk and sat down next to her in the vacant visitor's chair. "This isn't your fault."

Alex blinked, her eyes bright with emotion. "I should have anticipated this possibility. I knew better than to involve anyone else."

He leaned forward, bracing his elbows on his knees and wanting more than anything to take her hand, but knowing that he couldn't. Not yet, anyway. She was still wary of him.

"I think you should seriously consider at this point that you have an old enemy who has decided to settle the score. This case is pointing more and more in your direction."

She tossed the report aside, her anger flaring. "This is not about me. It's about my investigation into Marija's disappearance. If it were only about me why would he have killed Jasna?"

"You don't know that Jasna didn't kill herself," he offered, though his gut feeling told him otherwise. He had no proof at this point.

"Come on, Mitch, you know I'm right."

Every instinct told him that she was. But the evidence didn't add up.

Peg stuck her head in the door, interrupting his troubling thoughts. "It's Talkington for you," she said. "He's been trying to get you all morning."

Mitch had tried to call him back as soon as he and Alex returned to the office, but Talkington had been in some dead zone where cell phone service wasn't available. Mitch stood, reached across his desk and grabbed the receiver, then stabbed the blinking button for line one.

"Hayden."

"You're a hard man to track down."

"What've you got?" Mitch wasn't interested in exchanging pleasantries at the moment.

"A lot," Talkington mused. "First, I've got the final report on Jasna Bukovak. Detective Wells wasn't too keen on sharing, but I did a little arm twisting."

"Let's hear it." Mitch stilled, his senses edging to a higher state of alert.

"She definitely did not off herself. She had help," Talkington began. "Mixed in with all that soap under her nails was a trace of human flesh and since her body bore no such scratches, we know it isn't hers. Also lucky for us, the dumb bastard who sliced her was stupid enough to wash his hands, and obviously the scratches, afterward. We've got two different types of blood in the wastewater retrieved from the S-trap. One was the girl's, the other...who knows. There's also inconsistency in the depth of the wounds on her wrists to consider. One was shallow, the other deep, savagely so. Hell, the guy almost cut her hand off with that one. Even without the other evidence, it isn't likely she'd have done that to herself."

Mitch scrubbed a hand over his face. "Damn."

"Yeah," Talkington agreed.

Alex stared expectantly at him, but Mitch wanted to hear it all before he broke the news to her. She'd been right all along. On some level he'd known it, but... dammit...it seemed so unbelievable.

"Moving on to the sister, we can scratch Mayrija off Gill's kill list."

Mitch frowned. This was the one he'd been more sure of. "What do you mean?"

"The M.O.'s almost identical, whoever did her knew exactly what to do to make it look like Gill did it. But there was one very large inconsistency. She was shot once in the back of the head, execution-style with a small caliber handgun. A twenty-two. Looks like your cute little P.I. was right about Gill."

"Yeah, it does."

"Oh, one more thing," Talkington added, "Marija was pregnant. Second trimester, fifteen or sixteen weeks."

Mitch didn't really hear the rest of what Talkington had to say. He was too stunned. Alex had been right about all of it. He thanked the TBI agent and replaced the receiver in its cradle.

"I take it I was right about a few things," Alex said after reading his expression of disbelief.

"You were right about everything," he said, his voice oddly quiet. If Alex was right, then all the murders were connected. Miller, the Bukovak sisters and Stella and her roommate. And Alex would be next if Mitch couldn't stop the killer.

She tilted her head to study him more closely. "What did he say?"

Mitch rested his hip on the edge of his desk. "Jasna was murdered." He released a heavy breath. "Marija was pregnant, and she wasn't one of Gill's victims. Someone just wanted it to look that way. She was shot in the back of the head with a twenty-two."

Alex leveled a determined gaze on his. "He killed Miller and Saylor…Stella and Lorraine, too."

Mitch nodded. "Maybe."

She swore, a surprisingly scorching remark. "I can't believe you don't see the connection. He killed Marija because she was pregnant and threatened his lifestyle. When Jasna and I started digging around, he tried to kill us both. Miller probably just got in the way. Saylor definitely did. Stella and Lorraine are dead because he thought I was in that car."

Mitch gritted his teeth against the anger that rose inside him despite the evidence mounting. "By him I assume you mean Phillip."

Alex stood, her hands braced at her waist. "It has to be him. He had motive and he had means." She hesitated, then added, "Besides, he's done it before."

Mitch stiffened. "What are you talking about?"

"Fifteen years ago when Malloy was teaching law at Ole Miss, he had an affair with one of his students. When she got pregnant he tried to force her to take care of the problem. She was afraid so she took the money and ran.'' Alex stared up at him with fierce determination. ''This time he had a great deal more to lose or maybe Marija didn't cooperate, so he went too far.''

Mitch closed his eyes and cursed under his breath. He opened them once more and looked straight at her. ''How did you get this information?'' How could he not have known something like that about his own uncle?

''That's not important right now. You'll have to trust me when I say that my source is accurate.'' She hesitated, then went on, ''Have you been covering for your uncle?''

He couldn't quite read what he saw in her eyes now. Something between uncertainty and hope.

Mitch shook his head. ''Of course not.'' He searched her eyes. ''How could you think that?''

''Blood is thicker than water.''

''I'd do most anything to protect my family,'' he admitted. ''But not that.'' He frowned. ''Why didn't you tell me this before?''

''I didn't remember it until last night, and then I wasn't sure if I was remembering it correctly. But Ethan verified it this morning.''

As hard as it proved to swallow that reality, Mitch had to consider that the Colby Agency had likely meticulously verified their information.

''That still doesn't make him a killer,'' Mitch countered, his conviction waning a bit.

''Agreed. But it does make him a suspect.'' She pinned Mitch with an expectant gaze. ''If he's innocent he has nothing to fear from submitting to the DNA testing.''

She was right. If Phillip wasn't his uncle he wouldn't even hesitate. He'd sworn to uphold the law, and family or no, Mitch had to do his duty.

"All right. But I have to do this my way."

"What are we waiting for?"

PHILLIP STARED OUT the window for a long moment after Mitch told him what he knew. It grieved Mitch to the bone to have to do this. But Alex was right. Phillip had to be eliminated as a suspect. And this was the only way. The Bukovak girl lived in his house for six months, and if Alex was right about the rest, he had a great deal to lose if an illicit affair became public. The bottom line was that it was in Phillip's best interest to clear his name.

"One mistake in a lifetime of hard work," Phillip said, his usually booming voice now quaking. He turned back to Mitch. "I'm a stronger man now than I was fifteen years ago." He shook his head. "It was a mistake. Is everything I've worked for going to be taken away from me because of one mistake? I swear, Mitch, I didn't harm Marija. I treated her like my own daughter."

Mitch could see his pain. Every instinct told him that Phillip was telling the truth, but could Mitch trust his instincts in the matter? Was he allowing his heart to lead him as Alex had suggested?

"I'm not accusing you, Phillip," Mitch said solemnly. "I'm just advising you of the best course of action to protect yourself. If you're innocent you have nothing to worry about."

Phillip turned back to the window that overlooked his vast property. "Set it up."

"It's the right thing to do."

Mitch wondered why that assurance sounded so hollow in light of the pain he'd just dealt his uncle by making him relive a time in his past he'd obviously just as soon not remember.

"One last thing."

Phillip didn't turn around, but Mitch heard his sigh of defeat.

"And what is that?"

"I'll need to take a look at your truck." Phillip owned a brand-new four-wheel drive, extended cab, *black* truck.

"Well you can't. At least not right now," he added, his back still turned to Mitch.

Mitch's gut tightened. "Why is that?"

"I lent it to Roy."

Mitch felt a twinge of relief. "Ask him to bring it by the office when he returns it."

"Fine."

There was nothing else to say. Mitch stepped out of the study, closing the door behind him. Alex halted her pacing midstep at the sound of the door, she swung around to face Mitch.

"What did he say?"

"He told me to set it up."

Alex looked startled. "He did?"

"Are you surprised?" Mitch tamped down his ire. "I told you he was innocent."

"He could always skip town before the test," she suggested offhandedly.

Mitch gritted his teeth and snagged her by the elbow. "Let's go."

"What is *she* doing here?" a furious voice called out from the open front door.

He resisted the urge to cringe. Mitch had hoped to

be out of here before Nadine returned home from her weekly bridge game. "We're on our way out," Mitch assured her as he ushered Alex toward the door.

"I don't want her in my home!" Nadine shrieked. "I thought I made that clear before. She wants to destroy this family and I won't stand for it." Nadine shook her head, fury blazing in her eyes. "You bring her in my home again, Mitch Hayden, and I swear I won't be responsible for my actions."

"I'm—" he started an apology but Alex cut him off.

"Were you aware that your husband impregnated a young woman once before? How can you be so sure he didn't this time?"

Mitch swore. "Don't say another word." He nudged Alex toward the door.

She dug in her heels, stalling at the open door and staring at Nadine. "Don't you want to know the truth? Or maybe you're covering up the fact that you knew what was going on all along?"

Nadine's eyes glazed with hatred. "My husband is innocent," she said, seething. "And you, you're going to wish you'd never set foot in this town."

Chapter Twelve

Alex spent the entire afternoon going over her case-book. Or what was left of it. She shoved a fistful of hair behind her ear and blew out a disgusted breath. Nothing connected. But everything in her head...every cell of intuition told her that the answer somehow lay with Phillip Malloy.

Though his unexpected agreement to submit to DNA testing had thrown her for a bit of a loop, she wasn't convinced of his innocence. He was the center...it all started with him.

Dixon stepping out of Mitch's office and speaking to Peg captured Alex's frustrated attention. Alex watched as he took the file Peg retrieved for him and reentered Mitch's office. Mitch and Talkington were hunched over a small conference table, reports, interviews and crime scene photos spread across the table-top. Alex had declined the invitation to sit in on their brainstorming session. She'd looked at the reports when Talkington arrived. Nothing in that mass of compiled evidence held the answer.

The answer was locked inside her mind. Alex closed her eyes. And it just didn't want to come out.

The telephone extension on Dixon's desk rang. Alex

jumped at the sudden sound. Most calls came through Peg. The deputies rarely gave out their direct numbers. Maybe it was Ethan. She had given him the number. Alex rolled her neck to relieve the tense muscles and blew out a tight breath. "Okay, Alex, get a grip here."

She plucked up the receiver on the third ring. "Dixon's desk."

"I need to talk to you, Alex."

Die, bitch.

Alex jerked with the violent rush of memory. She pressed her fingertips to her temple to soothe the sudden, intense pounding there.

"You have to listen to me, Alex. I know what happened."

"Roy?" She rubbed her forehead, trying to erase the new and increasingly fierce pain streaking across her brow.

"I want to tell you everything, but I'm afraid…"

Alex closed her eyes and dragged in a deep, cleansing breath and let it out slowly. The pain subsided to a more tolerable level. "What are you afraid of, Roy?" Her voice was almost steady now. She pressed her hand to her chest and focused on slowing her racing heart.

"I can't talk about it on the phone. It's about my stepfather. You have to believe that I didn't know what he and Miller had planned."

Alex frowned. "Where are you? Why don't you come in to the office and we'll talk, just the two of us."

"No. I can't do that. I have to go—"

"Don't hang up," Alex blurted, desperate to keep him talking. "Please, don't hang up." He sounded distraught. The image of Jasna's lifeless body flashed before her eyes. "Tell me what you want me to do, Roy. I want to hear what you have to say. It's very important to me."

"I can tell you everything," he said quietly as if trying to prevent anyone from overhearing. "I was there. I know what Miller did." His voice cracked on the last two words.

"Okay." Anticipation sent adrenaline surging through her veins. This was it. "Why won't you come to the office?"

"I can't trust Mitch. He's known all along and he didn't do anything about it. He's covering for Phillip, just like I was. God, I can't believe I've let this happen." A desperate keening sound punctuated his words.

Alex stared at the receiver in her hand. Was he saying that Mitch was in on this? She couldn't believe that. "Are you sure about Mitch's involvement?" she prodded.

"To Mitch, family is everything," Roy said with clear disgust. "You know, *blood is thicker than water.*"

The words echoed inside her head. Jasna had said that same phrase to Alex.

"I can't stay on this line. I have to go."

Alex blinked away the unclear memory. "No, Roy, wait. Tell me where you want to meet. I'll come to you."

"You have to swear you won't tell Mitch."

"I won't say a word," Alex assured him.

"Meet me at the Down Under—in fifteen minutes. I'll tell you everything. I swear, Alex, I didn't know it would come to this." He made a choking sound that could have been a sob. "I didn't know."

"It's okay. We'll get it all worked out. Just stay cool."

Roy hung up. Alex slowly lowered the receiver back into its cradle. Roy was the key. She'd known that would be the case. She squeezed her eyes shut and banished the last, lingering remnants of the wicked headache that had lashed across her forehead only moments ago.

Roy was ready to talk. Alex opened her eyes and surveyed the reception area beyond the office she occupied. All she needed now was a set of wheels.

"I'M AS DISGUSTED as you are, Hayden, but the bottom line is that we don't have anything," Talkington concluded.

"None of it seems to tie together," Dixon agreed, indicating the mass of papers scattered between them on the conference table with a wide sweep of his hand.

They were right, Mitch conceded. The only way it all tied together was if Phillip was involved.

And Mitch just wasn't ready to accept that scenario quite yet, but he was definitely ready to see that the testing got done.

"If your P.I.'s right," Talkington began, leaning back in his chair, twirling a pen between the fingers of his right hand, "then it all started with Marija. She was murdered for whatever reason. Her sister was dissatisfied with the police's investigation so she hired a private agency." Talkington tapped the pen on the desk for emphasis. "That set the game in motion."

"Alex comes down here nosing around," Dixon offered, taking the ball and running with it. "She put out feelers all over town that she was looking into Phillip's background, all the while covertly checking into the

Bukovak girl's disappearance. The killer got wind of it and tried to do her. Maybe Miller knew something and planned to share it with Alex, the killer followed and *bam*," Dixon slammed his fist into his palm; Mitch flinched "he tried to off them both."

"But Alex survived," Mitch countered. He noted that Dixon carefully avoided accusing Phillip. Mitch hated to admit it, but he was grateful.

Talkington shook his head. "He was interrupted. Maybe by those kids who were camped nearby. Or maybe they showed up at that particular moment. He got spooked and ran, hoping he'd done enough damage to complete the job. When he realized she didn't expire, he made another attempt."

"Or three," Mitch added.

"But what about the drugs?" Dixon tossed out.

Mitch shrugged. "Could've been some kind of evidence Miller intended to bring in on another case. Could've been a bone to throw us off the scent left by the shooter."

"The plant sounds more logical," Talkington voted.

"This all sounds good in theory," Mitch said, "but how would our shooter know Gill's M.O.? The souvenir Gill took from his victims was never released to the public." Mitch cocked his head in question. "Was it?"

"No way." Talkington shook his head resolutely. "The only way anyone could have known those details is if a cop privy to the info spilled it."

"So we're saying our shooter is a cop now?" Dixon looked more than a little uneasy.

"No," Talkington denied. "We're saying he knows a cop who can't keep his mouth shut."

"Here's what we've got," Mitch summed up. "A

shooter who knows a cop, who drives a black SUV or truck and would have reason to want to kill Marija Bukovak.''

Dixon and Talkington remained silent, but their eyes spoke volumes. It all boiled down to Phillip Malloy. He drove a black pickup. He knew a cop or two and he had a definite connection to Marija. Not to mention he had a history of screwing around with young women.

Mitch shook his head and pushed out of his chair. ''It just doesn't sit right with me.'' Mitch rubbed his eyes with his thumb and forefinger. ''I can't see Phillip raping and murdering a girl who trusted him, or trying to kill Alex…or shooting Saylor like some kind of assassin. Not to mention forcing Stella's car off the highway.''

''Maybe he hired someone to do the dirty work,'' Dixon suggested quietly. Like Mitch, he looked distressed at his own words.

Mitch scrubbed a hand over his face. ''Maybe,'' he agreed halfheartedly. ''And maybe he's innocent.'' It troubled Mitch that he hadn't been able to reach Roy. Mitch needed to see that truck.

''The way I see it,'' Talkington declared, ''we can't be sure who the killer is without DNA comparison. That'll take time. And if Malloy isn't our man, we'll be back at square one.''

''Gee, that was enlightening,'' Mitch said sarcastically. ''Now tell us something we don't already know.''

Talkington scowled. ''Our killer wants Alex dead because he's afraid that anytime now she might remember who he is—''

''Oh, no.'' Mitch held up his hands stop sign fashion

and shook his head in emphasis of his words. "No way are we doing what you're about to suggest."

"To trap a killer you have to have bait." Talkington tapped the crime scene photos of Marija and Jasna Bukovak's dead bodies. "Are you going to let this guy go free? Alex will never be safe until he's caught anyway. She'd be the first to agree."

Mitch stabbed a finger in his direction. "We are not using Alex for bait. I won't allow it." He might have hoped at one time that keeping her close might lure the killer, but Mitch had been right by her side to protect her. No way was he letting Talkington use her. Not now...Mitch wouldn't risk it.

"This case getting a little personal?" Talkington asked smugly. "I'll talk to Alex myself if you don't. I'm certain she'll be game."

"Screw you, Talkington," Mitch growled.

"Do you want me to call her in?" Dixon ventured, looking from one to the other.

"Yeah," Mitch relented. "Call her in so I can tell her that Talkington wants to use her as bait for a killer."

"Anything to solve the crime," Talkington pointed out.

Mitch seethed. He wasn't quite sure how he would do it, but somehow he would prevent this little exercise from going down. This was his county.

Dixon scooted from his chair and hurried out of the office, no doubt happy to escape the tension.

Mitch glared at Talkington. "You know, sometimes I don't like you very much."

Talkington laughed. "There's only one difference between you and me, Hayden. I don't let my emotions get in the way of solving a case."

Dixon burst back into this office, his face as white as a sheet. "She's gone, Sheriff. And Peg is fit to be tied—her car is missing."

ALEX SAT in Peg's green sedan, waiting for Roy's arrival. She glanced at her watch for the seventh time and wished like hell that he would come on. When Mitch noticed she was missing, he'd be hot on her trail. And he'd be royally steamed.

She kept replaying Roy's words in her head. They seemed so familiar somehow. Her head still ached, just a continuous dull throb, but was annoying all the same. She should have taken some aspirin, but she hadn't taken the time. She didn't want to risk missing Roy. If he'd gotten here before her and she wasn't waiting, he might have taken off.

She checked her reflection in the mirror and noticed that the bruise on her cheek had finally faded completely. The wound on her forehead was healing nicely. There hadn't been much time to worry about her scrapes and bruises the past couple of days.

The image of the man in the ski mask zoomed before her eyes. The shouting in the background echoed in her ears. Fingers closing over her throat... *Die, bitch.*

The sound of a vehicle pulling up alongside her snapped Alex back to the present. Roy braked to a stop and climbed out of his truck. He waved uncertainly to her and waited for her to join him.

"Okay," Alex murmured to herself, "let's do it." She emerged from the car and rounded the trunk of Peg's car, hoping like hell that she didn't look as afraid as she felt. Another bout of déjà vu swamped her, as if she'd done this before.

"I'm glad you came, Alex," Roy said sincerely. "I

just couldn't keep this inside me any longer. I have to tell you what happened.'' He waved his arms in a magnanimous gesture. ''All of it.''

''All right. Do you want to talk here or is there someplace else you'd rather go. Someplace quiet where we can sit down and sort this out.''

Roy looked around nervously. ''First there's something I have to show you. It's important.''

Alex moved closer to him. He stood next to the open driver's side door as if he feared he might need to jump back inside and take off.

''See.'' He gestured inside the cab.

Wary, Alex eased closer still. She stopped directly in front of him and turned to look inside the cab at precisely the moment the color of the vehicle penetrated her consciousness.

An explosion of color burst before her eyes. Pain detonated inside her head. And then her world went as black as Roy's truck.

EVERYBODY AT THE DEPARTMANT was out looking for Peg's green sedan, including the custodian.

Mitch had to find Alex before the killer did. Peg had seen Alex talking on the phone shortly before she disappeared. Mitch could only assume that she'd set up a meeting with someone. Just to be sure, he drove by his uncle's office and made sure he was there. The move made Mitch feel like scum, but he wasn't taking any chances where Alex was concerned.

The radio in Mitch's Jeep crackled to life. ''Sheriff, we found it.''

''10-4, Willis, what's your 20?''

''Down Under. We'll stand by.''

Mitch made a U-turn. Five minutes later he skidded to a stop next to Peg's car.

"Everything's clean, Sheriff," Willis said as Mitch approached him. "No sign of foul play."

Mitch slowly circled the vehicle. Willis was right. Everything looked as it should. No sign of a struggle. No blood. He shuddered inwardly at the thought.

"You want me to call Talkington and Dixon?" Willis offered.

Dread pooled in Mitch's gut. He was too late. Alex had already made the connection.

"Yeah," Mitch said finally. "And see if you can locate Roy. I need to see him ASAP."

"Is he back from Nashville already?"

Mitch frowned. "What?"

Willis looked flustered. "You know, you sent him to Nashville to pick up that report from Wells."

"I didn't—" Mitch stopped dead in his tracks. Roy was a cop. Marija Bukovak had lived in the home of his parents. Roy had borrowed Philip's truck. And he knew all about Waylon Gill's case.

Ice-cold fear closed around Mitch, swelled inside him. He swallowed back the metallic taste of it.

"Willis, when did Roy tell you this?"

Willis scratched his head. "I don't know. Right after lunch maybe." He shrugged. "A couple hours ago, I guess. Is something wrong, Sheriff?"

"Put out an APB on Phillip's truck. Roy's driving it. I don't want anybody to approach him. I just want to know where he is."

"You think Roy's in some kind of trouble?"

Mitch struggled to take a breath. "Yeah. I think he's in big trouble."

Chapter Thirteen

Pain pierced the haze holding Alex just the other side of consciousness. She heard herself groan and felt a trickle of relief. She wasn't dead.

Her brain issued the command, but it felt like a lifetime before her eyes obeyed and slowly drifted open. There was hardly any light. She blinked, then squinted to make out any identifying details of her surroundings. A dank, musty smell registered in her senses. Where was she? Dark, nondescript walls lined with shelves surrounded her. A garage? Boxes, unused jars and other miscellaneous items she couldn't readily identify filled the shelves. A rustic staircase sagged against one wall. The floor beneath her felt cold and hard. A basement.

Her head throbbed viciously. Another groan rumbled up from her throat. The need to reach up and touch the hot spot to see if she was bleeding was overwhelming but her hands were tied behind her back. A frown dragged her lips downward…why was she tied up this way?

Heavy footfalls on the stairs echoed through the room. "Well, well, she's awake."

Roy. Looking inside the cab of his truck and getting

that blow to the head just as the color of his vehicle sank in slammed into her awareness now. Roy was the one who killed Stella and Lorraine.

You didn't say anything about killing her! Miller's frantic shouts zinged through Alex's head. Miller had tried to stop him when Roy had brutally beaten Alex. Miller's was the voice she'd heard in the background that night when the man in the ski mask had tried to kill her.

Roy.

Die, bitch.

But had he been trying to protect his stepfather or covering up his own doing? Phillip was the one with the skeleton in the closet. Roy had tried to kill her....

"It was you," she said with sudden understanding. "You killed Miller."

"That's right." Roy stood over her now, glaring down at her. "If I hadn't gotten interrupted that night, we wouldn't be having this little party now." He smiled smugly, clearly happy that it had taken so long for her to figure it out. "But, then again, I'm kind of glad it worked out that way. I'm planning to have myself a little fun before I stop your nosing around once and for all."

"Roy," Alex said, trying to keep reason in her voice and the fear out of it. She tried to sit up straighter, but the way her hands were tied and the fact that her legs had gone to sleep from sitting in such an awkward position for however long she'd been unconscious made movement impossible. "Do you really want to go to prison for the rest of your life or maybe even get the death penalty just so your uncle can get away with what he's done?" She looked into his eyes, beseeching him to see the futility of his actions.

"The DNA testing is going to nail him whether I'm there to testify to what I know or not," she went on. "You're too smart to be doing his dirty work." If she could make him think there was hope he might get away with what he'd already done if he stopped now, maybe he wouldn't kill her.

Roy laughed long and loud. "You don't know do you?" He laughed again. "Or maybe you knew and you just forgot. I'm not covering up for my uncle." He leaned toward her, waving the gun in his hand for emphasis. "I killed Marija."

Alex couldn't believe her ears. Not once had anyone she'd spoken with connected Roy with Marija. Alex closed her eyes and allowed the memories now rushing into her head to come freely. There had been no indication whatsoever that Roy had even seen the girl outside the Malloy home. Every clue Alex had uncovered before losing her memory pointed toward Phillip. She knew that with complete certainty. She'd been so intent on proving Phillip had something to do with Marija's disappearance that she hadn't looked to anyone else.

"Surprised?" Roy grinned. "Hell, yeah, you are. You thought you had this all figured out. With your silly notes and appointments to talk to people." He made a harrumphing sound. "I was too discreet. Nobody but Miller knew that Marija and I were involved. I have a reputation to uphold in this town. She was just a distraction for a couple of months."

Alex's stomach churned at how he'd misled, then mistreated the young girl who'd already suffered too many atrocities in her short life. Her existence had meant nothing to Roy. "Why didn't you just let her leave?" she demanded hoarsely. "You didn't have to kill her."

"Sure I did," he insisted haughtily. "She could have ruined my life. I know what happened to Phillip and I wasn't about to go through the same thing. No way. Every single day of his life he's had to worry that his one little indiscretion might come back to haunt him. Especially after he got into politics."

She had to get her hands loose. She didn't have a chance against him otherwise. She winced when the rope burned her wrists as she twisted within its hold.

He rubbed the muzzle of the weapon against his cheek. "I did her right here in this room," he said, as if the deed was somehow reverent.

Alex stilled and surveyed her surroundings once more. "Where are we?" she asked, as if it mattered.

"My house," he said offhandedly. "The basement."

"You picked her up at the airport?" Keep him distracted, she told herself.

He nodded. "I told her I'd decided we should be together. You know, get married, raise the kid, the works." He shook his head, those dark eyes gleaming with malice. "Did her up just like Gill. Better," he added with triumph. "I didn't get caught."

Alex frowned. So many of the details still didn't tie together. "If Miller was a good enough friend to be in on your affair with Marija, then why kill him?"

"Dumb bastard grew a conscience over the past couple of months. When you showed up nosing around, he got nervous. I couldn't have him saying anything stupid. So I told him that I was ready to talk to you, to tell you that the whole thing had been an accident, that I really didn't mean to kill her." Roy shook his head again, feigning sadness. "The fool fell for it. I planned on killing both of you, but a truckload of kids parked a short distance away and screwed me up." He leaned down and traced the wound on her forehead. "I was afraid to go back and make sure I'd done the job right. One of 'em might have seen me. The next morning I couldn't believe you'd survived that gunshot to the head."

The loud thumping rap music she'd remembered must have been the kids. Thank God for their timely arrival. Roy'd had to get away in a hurry. Those kids saved Alex's life. That and the fact that Roy's shot had only grazed her. Good thing he hadn't noticed.

"You shot Saylor," she said, the words more a rush of breath and memory than anything. God, he'd killed two of his fellow deputies without thought.

"Would've killed you, too, if you hadn't moved. Even planted the rifle in your room to make it look like you were working with the shooter. You're one lucky bitch, but that streak's about to end."

"You didn't have to run Stella's car off the road," Alex said, regret, hatred and anger mushrooming inside her. Stella hadn't known anything about any of this. Alex wanted to get loose and—

"You don't know anything! It's your fault," Roy said cruelly, his temper flaring. "If you'd died like you were supposed to have, none of this would have happened. Hell, I even tried to finish you off the morning we found you, but that stupid Willis kept hovering over you and asking if you were okay."

Die, bitch. The memory of Roy's hand over her mouth and nose trying to suffocate her exploded inside her head. He hadn't been trying to resuscitate her as Mitch believed.

Mitch...she was never going to see Mitch again. Alex trembled, then quickly grabbed back control. She had to think right now. All that stood between her and certain death at the moment was her ability to maintain Roy's interest.

"How do you expect to get away with this?" she suggested. "Mitch will figure it out."

"Blood's thicker than water," Roy taunted. "He won't do anything that'll jeopardize his family. I told Marija the same thing when she threatened to go to Mitch. Down here we stand by our kin."

"Why did you kill Jasna?" Alex asked suddenly, her mind jumping from one murder to the next. "She didn't know you were the one. She thought it was Phillip."

"She wouldn't let it go," he offered as if that explained everything and he'd been perfectly justified in what he did. "I couldn't risk one of you figuring it out."

"Well, Roy, I've got to admit, you're a pretty smart guy." She had to keep him talking. Her bonds were a little looser now. With any luck, in a few more minutes she might be free to at least attempt to defend herself. The longer she could distract him, the longer she would live.

When Mitch realized she was missing, would he come looking for her? The memory of the way he'd made love to her warmed her against the cold reality facing her now. He would come. She knew deep in her heart that Mitch wouldn't let her down. "You thought of everything, didn't you?" she said, forcing a respect she in no way felt into her tone.

Roy grinned. "I sure did. If I'd known how much fun killing would be, I'd have started a long time ago. There's nothing like watching a body twitch and squirm as you squeeze off the windpipe, blocking that life-giving air."

Alex shuddered inwardly. "I don't understand why you made that one mistake, though," she ventured hesitantly.

"What mistake?" he snapped. "I didn't make any mistakes."

"Gill never shot any of his victims," Alex reminded. "Why did you shoot Marija?"

Fury streaked across his face like lightning in a summer night sky. "You're lying! I didn't shoot the little slut. I strangled her just like Gill always did."

Alex dredged up a smile. "I can't fool you, can I, Roy?"

He crouched down and traced the line of her jaw with the nose of the thirty-eight. "Hell no. And don't you forget it either. Nobody fools me."

MITCH PARKED in Roy's driveway behind Phillip's truck. The driver's side door was open. He scanned the area around the house. The yard was clear. Mitch climbed out of his Jeep slowly, listening intently for any sound. The silence was deafening. The air too still for his liking.

He moved slowly toward the truck, his heart pounding so hard he could scarcely take a breath. He would not believe that anything had happened to Alex. He couldn't be too late. He clenched his teeth and refused to think about all that Roy had done right under Mitch's nose.

How could he have been so damned blind?

He surveyed the inside of the cab. No blood. That was good. His gaze jerked back to the shoe almost hidden under the seat. Mitch reached for the small navy loafer that belonged to Alex. She'd been wearing those shoes this morning.

Mitch tossed the shoe back into the vehicle and headed toward the house. He withdrew his weapon. If Roy had hurt...

He wouldn't think that way. He had to focus on finding her, then he'd deal with Roy.

As Mitch neared the porch he could see that the front door stood slightly ajar. He crossed the porch, his steps painfully slow and quiet so as not to give any warning. He eased the door open, not even breathing for fear of the whine the hinges might make. The door opened noiselessly.

Silence was all that greeted him as he moved across the living room. When he reached the hall he stopped long enough to identify the matching navy-blue shoe lying on the floor. A new wave of fear washed over him.

The kitchen, two bedrooms and a bathroom flanked the long hall. Mitch eased quietly to the next door. He peered into the kitchen. Nothing. The next door on that side of the hall stood open. Mitch tried to remember if it was a closet. He'd been here a couple of times, but couldn't recall what this door led to. But since it swung outward into the hall, it must be a...

Mitch reached the door and stared down the stairs it revealed.

Definitely not a closet.

A basement.

He didn't know the house had a basement.

Voices. One soft murmur—Alex. Thank God. Roy's laugh, a sick, evil sound.

Mitch had watched Roy go from a gangly teenager to a man with a burning desire to be a cop, and Mitch had facilitated that effort. When Nadine and Phillip had married ten years ago, Mitch had thought this ready-made family was the best thing that could have happened to his loner of an uncle.

Mitch couldn't have been more wrong.

Roy had killed at least two people, Stella and Lorraine. It followed that he wouldn't have killed them unless he had strong motivation, like wanting to cover up previous wrongdoing. Alex had been right on the money from the beginning. The whole thing started with Marija and snowballed from there.

Roy must have gotten her pregnant…then killed her.

Mitch pushed away the whirlwind of thoughts crowding his head. He had to focus. He'd been a fool not to trust Alex's instincts and look more closely at his own family's involvement in Marija's disappearance. He wouldn't be a fool now.

Sweat beaded on Mitch's forehead as he began his cautious journey down the rickety old stairs. He focused intently on not making a sound. Alex was speaking again, pleading with Roy to think about what he was doing. Mitch's heart squeezed at the sound of her fearful voice. Two more steps and he would be able to see.

Slowly, quietly, he eased down the two steps that would allow him to see the basement in its entirety. Mitch's heart slammed against his sternum when his gaze landed on Alex, her eyes wide with fear as Roy's fingers tightened around her throat. He was crouching over her, a thirty-eight in his right hand.

"I tried to throw you off track by tearing those pages from your notebook and framing Mitch, but you just wouldn't back off. Now I'm gonna do you just like I did her," Roy boasted. "Then I'll bury you in the middle of nowhere. When they find you they'll think old

Gill's got himself a fan. They'll call it a copycat murder.''

Roy pressed the barrel of his weapon against Alex's temple. Mitch's heart seemed to stop completely then. He managed to get down another couple of steps, his weapon leveled on Roy.

"Gill might even be flattered." Roy laughed cruelly. "And you'll be dead."

Alex tried to squirm away from him.

Mitch's whole body jerked with reaction.

"Don't worry," Roy taunted. "I'm going to take my time. You won't feel most of it. Then you'll be dead and I won't even have fired my weapon. No one will hear, just like they didn't hear when I did Marija in this very room cause I didn't make a sound. Not a single sound."

Alex opened her mouth to scream. Roy clamped his hand down hard over her mouth. "Don't bother," he muttered hotly. "No one's coming for you. No one believes you."

"Drop your weapon, Roy." Mitch was still several steps from the bottom of the stairs, but he had a perfect bead on Roy.

"Go away, Mitch," Roy said flatly without even looking in his direction. "You don't want to see this."

"I said, drop your weapon," Mitch commanded. "Don't make me kill you, Roy."

His muzzle still jammed into Alex's temple, Roy's gaze darted to Mitch. "You gonna take her side over mine? If she hadn't come here none of this would have happened. It's her fault Miller and Saylor are dead. She left me no choice. *You* left me no choice." The pitch of his voice grew higher with each word. He was losing it. And Mitch had to stop him before he did.

"Just toss your weapon aside, Roy," Mitch said patiently. "And we'll talk about this."

Roy shook his head. "No way. I'm killing her. She's the only one who can prove what really happened. I can't let her live. She's got you under some kind of spell."

"Think about your mother, Roy," Mitch urged. "Think how devastated she'll be if I have to shoot you."

Roy blinked twice as if considering Mitch's words and hesitated. Then a sick grin slid across his lips. "You're not going to shoot me, Cousin Mitch," he said, addressing Mitch the way he did as a lanky kid. "I'm family."

A new kind of tension tapped its way up Mitch's spine.

"Now go on," Roy urged, "and let me do what I gotta do."

"I can't do that," Mitch countered. "You know I can't.

Roy whipped around, his weapon leveling on Mitch. "Then die with her."

Alex screamed, the sound underscoring the two shots, one right after the other. Roy looked startled, the shot Mitch fired having given him a third eye and a ticket straight to hell. He slumped to the basement floor.

Mitch lay motionless at the bottom of the stairs. Alex kicked away from Roy's body and struggled to her feet. She had to get to Mitch. Had to help him. As she stumbled across the room she jerked and tugged to get her hands free.

She dropped to her knees beside his too-still body. "Mitch." She jerked frantically at her bonds.

"Mitch!" she cried, hoping to rouse him. Blood had soaked his shirt. The wound was low on his left side. "Oh, God."

She tugged harder. One hand pulled free. Thank God. Thank God. She shook her other hand free of the rope and checked his pulse. Then took a better look at the wound. Panic tightened around her throat. The bleeding hadn't slowed. Thankfully, it appeared that the fall down the stairs and not the gunshot had rendered him unconscious.

But his neck or back could be broken. She had to get help. What was she waiting for? He could bleed to death before she pulled herself together.

Alex raced up the stairs, stumbling twice before reaching the top. She rushed through the house until she found the phone. She snatched up the receiver and depressed 9-1-1.

"I need help," she blurted as soon as the operator had finished her spiel.

"What is the nature of your emergency?"

Alex wanted to scream. "He's been shot. He's bleeding badly. Please hurry!"

"Calm down, ma'am, we'll get someone on the way right now."

It hit Alex then that she didn't even know where she was. "I don't know the address!"

"It's all right, ma'am. We've got you. We know where you are and someone is on the way."

"Okay. Okay." Alex closed her eyes and tried to calm herself. But it didn't work. She knew the drill. Help was on its way.

"Are you safe, ma'am? Is the shooter still there? Do you need to get out of the house?"

Mitch. Alex had to help Mitch until the paramedics

arrived. Alex dropped the phone and flew back down the stairs.

He still hadn't moved.

She knelt beside him and placed her hand over the wound. There was so much blood. She pressed hard to try and slow it. The warm life-giving fluid oozed between her fingers. Just like Saylor. She hadn't been able to help him. Alex sucked in a shuddering breath. She had to try. She had training for this.

But this was Mitch.

The man she loved.

Chapter Fourteen

By midnight that night Mitch was resting comfortably. Alex watched him sleep now, so very thankful that his prognosis was good. The internal injuries were very minor compared to what could have been. The bump on his head was only a mild contusion. The CT scan had revealed nothing of concern and Mitch had no glitches in his thought processes or his memory as far as the doctors could tell.

Alex closed her eyes and sighed. She was so tired and relieved. Although she still had not regained her complete memory, little bits and pieces were missing here and there, most of it was back. The afternoon prior to Miller's murder she had just connected Roy and the Malloys. When she questioned Miller about Roy, Miller broke. He promised to tell her everything that night.

After arriving at the rendezvous point, Miller had behaved strangely. He kept telling her that it wasn't his fault. That Roy had set up everything. That he'd spread the lies about Marija's cocaine use. That he'd even had Miller passing messages to Marija at the club so it would look like he and Marija were together. Miller hadn't realized until later that Roy had only used him to keep from being seen in public with the girl. Miller hadn't known exactly what Roy had done until Jasna came looking for her sister.

Alex now clearly remembered Roy joining her and Miller that night. Miller had been as startled as she by the ski mask Roy wore. He had said his hellos and then proceeded to beat Alex unmercifully. Miller had tried to stop him, but Roy had warned him to stay back. There was nothing after that except the glimpse of memory where someone, Roy she knew now, had held her hand and made her fire her weapon. Then the horror of Miller's dead body behind the steering wheel of his car. She vaguely recalled being loaded into the passenger seat opposite Miller, followed by the weapon firing at her, the loud rap music, then nothing. Everything after that was still hit or miss.

But Alex remembered everything prior to the shooting, including that one dinner with Mitch. Though she'd never been a believer in love at first sight, something had definitely happened between them that night. Something much deeper than just attraction. And even after she'd become his suspect, Mitch couldn't push away what he felt for her.

Alex opened her eyes and smiled, her gaze blurring with tears. Mitch loved her, and she loved him. She wasn't sure what in the world they would do about it, but she was sure of the love.

She glanced at the clock on the wall. Zach should have been here by now. When she'd talked to Victoria to give her the news while Mitch was in recovery, Zach had insisted on coming down to be with Alex. She'd tried to talk him out of it, but that wasn't happening.

Alex rubbed her eyes and then touched the lump on her head. Dr. Reynor had insisted on checking her out while Mitch was in surgery. But her latest bang on the head hadn't done any further damage. She hoped she'd had her share of head lumps for a while.

A soft knock on the door brought Alex to her feet. She hurried to the door to greet Zach. Ethan stuck his head in. He noted that Mitch was sleeping and said, "Step out in the hall for a minute, Al."

"Where's Zach?" she whispered back as she slipped from the room. Not that she wasn't glad to see Ethan, but Zach had been so adamant about coming himself.

"You holding up okay?" Ethan gave her a quick hug.

"I'm fine. But what happened to Zach?" She chewed her bottom lip, worry creasing her brow. This wasn't like Zach.

Ethan lifted a skeptical brow. "You mean you're not glad to see me?" A devilish grin kicked up one corner of his mouth.

Alex couldn't help her own smile. Ethan was one of a kind. He was the only Colby investigator who got away with wearing long hair and overly casual clothing. Ethan Delaney was strictly a jeans kind of man. It drove Ian Michaels, Victoria's second in command, crazy. But Victoria allowed it because Ethan was good.

He was an expert marksman with former military training and he could charm the socks off any female still breathing.

Alex sighed. "Of course I'm glad to see you." She chucked him on the shoulder. "I guess I'm just tired and a little punchy."

"You look tired," he said, searching her weary face. His expression grew suddenly solemn. "I hate to have to add a new worry to your load."

She'd known it. "What is it, Ethan? Has something happened to Zach?" Her heart stumbled into overdrive.

Ethan shook his head. "He's fine, but his mother had a heart attack and he had to rush home."

"Oh, no." Tears gathered behind her eyes. "She's the only family he has left."

"I talked to Victoria after I landed in Nashville. Mrs. Ashton is stable. She's going to be all right."

"Thank God." Alex ran her fingers through her hair. Her head ached and she was totally exhausted. She wasn't up for any more bad news tonight. She was barely hanging on to her composure as it was.

Ethan glanced at his watch. "Look, why don't you go get a few hours sleep and I'll wait with the sheriff." He handed Alex his cell phone. "I'll call you if anything changes."

Alex stared at the phone in her hand, then shook her head. "I can't leave him."

Ethan peeked into the room again. "Look, he's asleep, there's no reason you can't go for a while. I'll call you if anything at all changes. Or if he wakes up."

Alex started to protest, but then realized the futility of it. Victoria trained her investigators too well. Never Say Die was their motto. And Alex was far too tired to keep up.

"All right. I'll go to Mitch's house and get a few hours' sleep. But you have to promise me you'll call if he wakes up. I don't want him to wake up and not find me close by."

Ethan grinned. "So it's that way, is it?"

Alex snatched the car keys he offered next. "Yeah," she retorted. "It's exactly that way."

"It's a white sedan parked out front."

"Thanks. I'll go for a little while then." She peeked through the door one last time. She didn't want to leave, but she did need a bath and some sleep. She pointed a finger at Ethan. "Call me."

He gave her a mock salute.

On the drive to Mitch's house along dark, quiet streets, Alex had herself a good cry. Jasna, Marija and the child she'd been carrying were dead. Roy had taken four other lives to cover his tracks, and would have killed her if Mitch hadn't come to her rescue.

She released a shuddering breath. *Mitch.* How was she supposed to go back to Chicago and pretend she hadn't fallen in love with him? Although he hadn't actually told her that he loved her, she knew he felt deeply for her. It had started that first night, just as it had for her. A memory her brain had buried with the concussion and traumatic events of the shooting, but her heart wouldn't let her forget.

Alex parked the rental car in front of the dark house that belonged to Mitch. She shivered with apprehension. "Get over it, Alex, it's done. Roy is dead. There's nothing else to be afraid of here."

PAIN SEARED his gut. Mitch groaned and slowly roused. His eyes opened even slower. He blinked several times to focus. He tightened his fingers into a fist and felt the sting of the IV needle and the barrage of tape holding it in place on the back of his right hand. He lifted his left hand and touched his parched lips.

Man, he was thirsty.

The events that had taken place in Roy's basement rushed through his head like a runaway train.

Roy was dead.

Mitch closed his eyes once more against that reality. He'd had to kill him. He wondered fleetingly how Phillip and Nadine were taking the news. To lose their son was bad enough, but to discover that he'd been a murderer a half-dozen times over made it unbearable. The memory of the kid Roy had once been bloomed in Mitch's mind next. How could he have grown up to be a killer? How could Mitch not have seen it coming?

It didn't make sense.

The one thing in all this that did make sense was his feelings for Alex. He'd never felt this deeply for any woman. He loved her. The thought startled him just a little. He hadn't considered that he might feel this way any time soon. Falling in love and settling down had always been off in the future. He hadn't had time for it.

But fate had intervened and along came Alex.

She'd stayed right by his side all night. He turned to look at her now, a smile tugging at his lips. That smile died a sure and swift death when his gaze landed on a stranger—a male one at that.

"Where's Alex?" Mitch asked, his voice rusty.

The man jerked awake and straightened in his chair. "Alex? I sent her to catch a little shut-eye. She looked ready to drop." He stretched, then extended his hand. "I'm Ethan Delaney from the Colby Agency."

Mitch waved his hand away since shaking wasn't so easy considering his current circumstances. "I remember the name. You were in on the conference call."

"That was me," Delaney agreed.

"What happened to Ashton?" Mitch wondered why he hadn't come running as soon as he heard what had happened. The thought of him comforting Alex sent another kind of sensation searing through Mitch.

"He had a family emergency."

Mitch felt immediately contrite. "That's too bad."

"His mother had a heart attack," Delaney explained. "But she's going to be fine."

Mitch nodded. "Good."

"I'm supposed to call Alex when you wake up." Delaney stood and picked up the receiver from the telephone on the bedside table.

"It's late," Mitch said, making him hesitate. "She might be asleep."

Delaney considered that, then said, "She hasn't been gone that long." He chuckled. "Besides, there's no way I'm going to face her wrath if she finds out I didn't call. I have to work with the woman on a regular basis."

That last remark left Mitch feeling empty. Delaney was right. Alex worked in Chicago. She loved her job. No matter what they thought they felt for each other. It wasn't likely that she would give up her life for one with him. And couldn't the same be said of him? Mitch couldn't see himself doing anything else but sheriffing in Raleigh County. How long would a long-distance relationship last?

Not long enough.

"Here you go." Ethan handed Mitch the receiver.

"Alex." His heart pounded at just the sound of her name on his lips.

"Hey, you feeling okay? I'll be back at the hospital in ten minutes."

Mitch shook his head, then frowned at his own stupidity. She couldn't see him. Obviously his brain was still fuzzy. "No, you rest. There's no need for you to come back before morning."

"I'm not sure I can stay away that long," she murmured.

The soft, caring sound of her voice reached out to

him. Soothed that emptiness he felt inside at the thought of losing her forever.

"Do you know what I'm doing?"

Mitch tensed. "No. Tell me." He stole a glance at Delaney who was thumbing through an old magazine.

"I just took off all my clothes," she said with a sigh. "The tub is full of steaming water and I'm about to sink into it."

She moaned as she obviously lowered her body into the water. Mitch almost groaned at the erotic sounds and the images they created in his mind.

"That feels so good," she whispered.

Mitch could imagine her reclining in his tub, her slender body enveloped by the warm water. Her dusky nipples would harden and stand at attention. Her eyes would close in pleasure.

He swallowed hard. "Wish I were there," he rasped.

"Me, too. Hmm."

"Good night, Alex," he said softly, his body becoming aroused in spite of his injuries.

"'Night," she murmured, then hung up.

Mitch closed his eyes and relished the lingering images of Alex completely nude and in his arms instead of in the tub.

"Everything okay?"

Delaney took the receiver from Mitch's hand and placed it back in its cradle.

"Yeah. Everything's great."

...I won't even have fired my weapon.

The memory of Roy's words burst into Mitch's thoughts. He blinked with the force of it. Roy had said that he'd killed Marija quietly. No one had heard. He hadn't even fired his weapon. But that was impossible. Marija was shot once in the back of the head.

Fear pooled in Mitch's chest. If Roy didn't shoot the girl, then someone else did. Someone working with Roy? That didn't make sense. Someone trying to cover for Roy?

"Help me up!" Mitch jerked the tape from his hand, swearing profusely at the pain. He removed the IV needle a little more carefully.

"What the hell are you doing, Hayden?" Ethan was standing beside him now.

"Help me up, dammit." Mitch struggled to sit up, but the pain was so violent he fell back against his pillow with the power of it.

"You can't go anywhere like this," Delaney argued. "Do you need a nurse?"

"Look," Mitch said harshly, his breath coming in ragged spurts to fight the renewed surge of pain he'd caused, sweat had popped out on his forehead. "I think there may be someone else involved in all this. I don't have time to explain why or how, just trust me. Something's wrong. Now help me get out of here. We have to get to Alex now."

Delaney halted Mitch's struggle to sit up. "You stay right here. If you think Alex might be in danger, tell me how to get to your house and I'll go check on her."

Mitch grabbed him by the arm and pulled himself upward, gritting his teeth against the agony. "Get my clothes. Hurry!"

Apparently seeing that there was no changing his mind, Delaney nodded. "Okay. Okay."

"Hurry," Mitch commanded when the guy didn't move fast enough for him. He reached into the drawer of the table and took out his weapon. "We have to hurry," he repeated. He had a very bad feeling that this wasn't over.

ALEX HAD almost drifted off to sleep in the warm water's embrace when a sound prodded her eyes open. She frowned and listened for the sound again. The occasional drip of the faucet was all that disrupted the otherwise quiet.

She tried to recover that relaxed feeling, but it wouldn't come. That annoying sixth sense kept urging her to get out of the tub and check out the house. She'd locked the door when she came in. That was habit. She lived in the city and unlike the folks around here, she never left her door unlocked.

Disgusted with her paranoia but knowing she might as well get out and do what she had to do, Alex emerged from the water and dried herself off. Thankfully she'd had the foresight to bring her nightshirt into the room. She pulled it on, but didn't take the time to pull the pins from her hair.

Feeling just a little foolish, but determined to satisfy that little voice deep inside her, Alex eased the door open and slipped into the cool hall. She shivered as the much cooler air cloaked her still slightly damp skin.

Moving soundless, she made her way into the kitchen and found it empty. She breathed a sigh of relief and tiptoed back into the hall. The sight of Nadine Malloy didn't register at first. Alex blinked and peered again, only to find Nadine still there, a small handgun aimed at Alex.

"You killed my son."

The woman's eyes were swollen and red from crying. Her hand shook slightly, but she quickly steadied it. "And now I'm going to kill you."

"Wait, Mrs. Malloy," Alex said carefully. "I didn't kill your son. He was trying to kill me and—"

"Don't try and explain it away," she spat. "You

killed him. You should never have come here and started digging around in things that weren't your business.''

''But I had to try to find my client's sister,'' Alex reasoned, all the while grappling to think of the best way to dodge the bullet no doubt about to come her way.

''The little whore.'' Nadine's eyes snapped with fury. ''I didn't want her. It was Phillip's idea. The stupid bastard. He knew better than to bring that kind of temptation into our home. He'd already made that mistake once. What kind of example was he setting for my son when he couldn't stop fawning over the little tramp?''

''I'm sure Mr. Malloy didn't intend things to happen this way,'' Alex offered, hoping to avoid saying anything that might send the woman the rest of the way over the edge.

She made a dismissing sound. ''How could he expect my Roy to resist when he hadn't all those years ago?'' She shook her head. ''It was all his fault, but he's already paid for his mistake. Now it's time for you to pay for yours.''

Had she killed Phillip Malloy? Fear raced up Alex's spine and tingled in her scalp. After Nadine killed Alex, would she try to hurt Mitch as well? Ethan was with Mitch. He wouldn't allow Nadine to harm Mitch.

''If you do this, Nadine, you'll be sorry,'' Alex urged. ''Think. You're upset right now. Do you really want to go to prison for killing me? It won't bring Roy back. Phillip needs you.'' If he was even still alive.

She laughed, a sound that could only be called off-kilter. ''He doesn't need anybody anymore and neither will you.'' She steadied her aim. ''Besides,'' she added, "I've already killed once before and didn't get caught."

Alex resisted the urge to run like hell. "You can't mean that."

"I knew he wouldn't do it right, just like he didn't do you right." Nadine closed one eye, focusing on Alex's head. "When I found out what he'd done to Marija, I went to where he'd buried her to make sure he'd done the job right." She relaxed her stance for a moment. "Just like I thought, he'd bumbled it. She was still alive, barely." Nadine shrugged. "But I took care of that. I warned him he'd better find a way to get rid of you, but he just couldn't manage it. But that's all right because now—" she resumed her bead on Alex "—I'm going to take care of you, too."

The sound of a weapon firing exploded in the hall. Alex jerked at the loudness of it, then stared down at herself to see where she'd been hit.

There was no blood.

No hole.

Nothing.

She looked up and Nadine lay on the floor. Mitch, standing on the threshold of the open front door, lowered his weapon and slumped against the doorframe. His free hand went to his injured side.

Alex ran to him, dodging Nadine's motionless body as she went.

"What are you doing here?" She had to touch him. His face, his chest, his arms. "Are you all right?"

He nodded weakly. "I am now."

"Why the hell didn't you tell me you had a dead bolt on your back door?"

Alex swung around to find Ethan coming out of the kitchen rubbing his right shoulder.

"You'll need a new door, by the way," he added sheepishly.

How could she have missed the sound of him breaking down the back door? Alex shook her head. She supposed when faced with the prospect of certain death, one tuned out everything else, including Mitch opening the front door. But Nadine had been between her and the door, she rationalized.

Alex frowned, still not understanding exactly what had happened.

"How did the two of you get here?"

Ethan nodded toward Mitch. "When the nurse came in and caught us trying to leave, he deputized her and took possession of her vehicle."

Alex laughed, suddenly feeling hysterical. She turned back to Mitch who was looking a little too pale to suit her. He was wearing his own jeans and a borrowed lab coat. "Tell me he's joking."

Mitch shook his head. "He's not. I had to get here. I remembered what Roy said about not using his weapon when he killed Marija and I knew there had to be somebody else involved." He sighed. "I just didn't expect it to be Nadine."

He was right. Roy had been shocked at Alex's suggestion that he'd shot Marija. With all that had happened, Alex had simply forgotten that part. She'd been too concerned with Mitch's survival.

Nadine's words suddenly reverberated in Alex's ears. "I think she's killed Phillip."

Mitch tried to straighten, but sagged back against the doorframe. "Get someone over there," he said to Ethan, then rattled off the address.

While Ethan made the 9-1-1 call, Alex carefully slipped her arm around Mitch's waist. "Come on, I'm getting you back to the hospital. Ethan can take care of things here.''

Mitch didn't argue. When they'd made the arduous journey back to the borrowed car, he paused before getting inside.

He stared directly into Alex's eyes, the light from the car's interior highlighting his face. ''I don't want this to be over.''

A broad smile slid across her face as tears welled in her eyes. She tiptoed and kissed Mitch on the cheek, being careful not to get too close. When she would have pulled away, his fingers curled around her neck and he deepened the kiss. The feeling of rightness, of love and need and desire filled her so completely that she couldn't hold back those tears.

When he at last released her, she looked deep into his amazing blue eyes and said, ''It's never going to be over. I love you, Mitch.''

He swiped a tear from her cheek. ''I love you.''

''Are you going back to the hospital?'' Ethan yelled from the porch. ''Or are you just going to stand around here until he falls over? The nurse gave me forty-five minutes to get him back there.'' He waved a pair of jeans and shoes at Alex. ''I thought you might need these.''

Alex blushed as she thought of what she was wearing—nothing but a nightshirt. She quickly pressed one last kiss to Mitch's lips. As brave as he was being, the pain was showing on his face. ''We'd better get you back. I want you well—soon. I have big plans that include you in top physical form.''

''In that case,'' he said softly. ''I'm definitely ready to go.''

Epilogue

"She's absolutely adorable, Ian." Victoria admired the newest photographs of Ian's baby daughter, then passed them back to the doting father. The child truly was precious, but it pained Victoria to think of all she'd missed in her own life.

Pushing that useless train of thought aside, she focused on the two men seated across her desk. She had business to attend to. There was no time for loitering in the past. "Is Zach still coming back tomorrow?" she asked of Ian, her second in command.

"Yes. His mother is doing well now and he sees no reason to stay any longer."

"Good." Victoria took a moment to study the two men before her. Ian Michaels, classically handsome, his dress and demeanor just as classic. She shifted her gaze to Ethan Delaney, the exact opposite in every respect. Except in looks. Ethan was equally handsome, in a more rugged, outdoorsy way.

"And Alex is enjoying her vacation?" Victoria directed this question to Ethan.

He grinned. "She's having a great time, though I don't think she'll be rested when she gets back."

Victoria would have to see that every effort was taken to facilitate Alex's relationship with Mitch Hayden. The Colby Agency could not afford to lose her. She was far too valuable. But, Victoria was immensely glad that Alex and Mitch had found each other. That kind of love didn't come along every day.

The image of Lucas Camp slipped into her mind. His slow smile and knowing eyes. Victoria blinked, banishing her longtime friend. This was not the time and place to savor thoughts of Lucas.

"Very well then, where are we with our caseload considering Alex's absence?"

"Everything is under control," Ian assured her. "We have a couple of potential cases that I plan to pass to Ethan. I feel he's best suited for the client environment."

Victoria turned to Ethan. "You're closed out on your latest case?"

"Sure am. Filed the report this morning." He grinned that lopsided gesture that Victoria fancied, as did most females she felt certain. "You know I don't beat around the bush," he added in that cocky Delaney tone.

"Excellent." Victoria turned back to Ian. "Anything else?"

"I had a call from Sloan this morning," he began, surprising Victoria. She hadn't heard from Trevor Sloan since his marriage to Rachel.

"Is everything all right?"

Ian nodded. "He picked up a rumor that involved the Colby Agency. He thought we should be aware that Leberman is making inquiries regarding some of our cases."

Leberman. Now there was a name Victoria could have gone the rest of her life without hearing again. She pushed away the inkling of fear that accompanied the memory of the man. He was evil incarnate. He'd cost the Colby Agency two good men. But that had been when she'd first taken over after James's death. She was much savvier in this business now. The Leberman situation would not happen again.

"There are two unsolved cases in the files that remotely involve Leberman," she said thoughtfully. "Pull those files and see what you can find, Ian. Have Quinn work up a study on both. I want to know where the players are and what they're doing. If Leberman is asking questions, then we should be prepared for the worst."

Ian lifted one dark, perceptible brow. "Quinn will be pleased."

William Quinn was the agency's new intern. A former Chicago P.D. rookie cop, he'd shucked the uniform and returned to law school with a burning desire to change the way justice was levied. At twenty-two, he was hungry and relentless. If there was anything else to find in those old, unsolved cases, Quinn would find it.

"Keep me updated on his progress," she told Ian. "I'll call Sloan and thank him for the heads-up on Leberman."

"Who's Leberman?" Ethan asked, looking from one to the other.

"Bad news," Victoria told him frankly. "Very bad news. If Leberman had his way the Colby Agency would be destroyed."

"It's our job," Ian said confidently, "to see that he doesn't have his way."

Victoria smiled. "Indeed."

The Colby Agency employed the best—like the two men seated before her. *No one* could touch the Colby Agency.

* * * * *

Be sure to catch Zach's story, next month
available from our friends at
Harlequin American Romance.
THE MARRIAGE PRESCRIPTION
by Debra Webb.

Who was she really?

Where Memories Lie

GAYLE WILSON

AMANDA STEVENS

Two full-length novels of enticing, romantic suspense—by
two favorite authors.

They don't remember their names or lives, but the two
heroines in these two fascinating novels do know one thing:
they are women of passion. Can love help bring back the
memories they've lost?

*Look for WHERE MEMORIES LIE in July 2002—
wherever books are sold.*

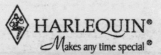

HARLEQUIN®
Makes any time special®

Visit us at www.eHarlequin.com

BR2WML